MW00878844

A WINDOW IN AN UNLIKELY PLACE

Travis Lambert

Cover Illustration and Frontispiece
Copyright © 2015 Rashie Rosenfarb

Library of Congress Control Number: 2015917238
CreateSpace Independent Publishing Platform, North Charleston, SC

ISBN: 1514802090
ISBN-13: 978-1514802090

For Walter Hooper.

And for a very special group of students
in the Deep South
who, at one time,
comprised my fifth grade Latin class.

"*Spell* means both a story told,
and a formula of power over living men."

J. R. R. Tolkien, *On Fairy-Stories*

CONTENTS

CONTENTS

WHEREIN THE NARRATOR IS INTRODUCED

This is a story about a girl named Ada who disliked stories. Actually, most of it is about another story—which has magic in it—that was told to her and her cousins by Uncle Daniel when the whole family got together for an otherwise boring vacation. This took place in a cabin in the woods out in the middle of Nowhere, Michigan; so Uncle Daniel had a lot of time to tell his story—which is peopled by dwarves—and he would need all that time to get Ada to change her mind about stories.

Our story begins in a huge cabin in a forest with Ada sitting on the hearth of the fireplace. She was dying of boredom, as anyone could see by her folded arms and tapping fingernails, which were drying after their most recent coat of nail polish. Her smartphone had no service out there. There was nothing on TV, because the signal came through an Iron Age artifact called an antenna, which, Ada was sure, you could still buy at an antique store for the price of a rabbit and two pigeons. And there were no magazines. There were only books about home improvement and hunting, and Westerns. Ada only liked reading magazines. And there were no movies that didn't have Clint Eastwood or John Wayne in them. Ada only liked romantic films.

Ada was withering like a leaf and sighing miserably, listening to the cars come down the snowy, winding lane from the main road. She heard the sound of engines turning off and the car doors opening and shutting. The problem was that she had no cousins her own age, and none of the adults were any fun—none except Uncle Daniel, though she was now too old in her own eyes to admit it. But she didn't know if he was coming. As the afternoon wore on there was an increase of noise, and there was a lot of coming and going, and the piling of luggage and groceries. Ada's cousins arrived: Andy and Melissa, twins (both of them), who were the closest to Ada in age, but they were still three years younger (and probably always would be). The only other cousin to come on this vacation was an infant, and Ada, unlike other girls, wasn't fond of babies. The baby's mother was reading Dr. Seuss to him, and meanwhile the noise increased downstairs. There were a lot of adults, and there was a lot of laughter. There were laughs of all kinds: big laughs, small laughs, high laughs, low laughs, laughs of all speeds, even very, very slow laughs.

Ada sat on the edge of the dead fireplace, cold, full of self-pity, waiting for her parents to notice her, waiting for someone to start a fire, waiting for something— anything!—to happen. And finally something did happen, the very something Ada was hoping would happen. Uncle Daniel arrived.

Her uncle's rickety old truck coughed, sputtered, and wheezed down the driveway, and the brakes squealed to a stop. There is a story that Mrs. Uncle Daniel used to tell (when she was still alive) about their dog (when it was still alive). The dog, she used to say, could hear Uncle Daniel's truck coming from a long way off. The muffler had fallen off years ago, which made the truck very loud. The twist of the story is that they lived near a small airport, and every time an airplane flew overhead the dog ran to the fence to see if Uncle Daniel was coming home.

Mrs. Uncle Daniel was always telling him that he should get a new truck, but, as he told her and all the police who gave him tickets for having no muffler, he couldn't bring himself to get rid of something he'd lived with for so long. His wife, of course, could understand that, and the police came to understand it too, for by now Uncle Daniel knew the entire police force of Nowhere County, and they had stopped writing him tickets.

Now, of course, all he had was his truck, and he would certainly have traded it to get Mrs. Uncle Daniel and his dog back, or even just one of them (preferably his wife). But Uncle Daniel preferred most of all not to talk about it, and so we shall respect his wishes.

When Ada heard Uncle Daniel's truck, her ears pricked up, and Andy and Melissa ran to the window as if they'd heard the ice cream truck. "Uncle Daniel's here!" announced Andy, and Melissa clapped her little hands and jumped with glee. Ada wanted to get up too, but she didn't. Her cousins pressed their faces against the sliding glass door of the balcony that one of the aunts had just cleaned. They looked down and watched the headlights turn off. The engine roared and then went silent, except for a coughing sound like a death rattle. It made one wonder—or at least it made Ada wonder—whether it would ever start again.

After a few minutes Uncle Daniel's hat appeared as he came up the stairs, and he hardly had time to take off his long coat and put down his suitcase before Andy and Melissa tackled him. In fact, he had no time—he dropped the suitcase. "Well, hello there!" said Uncle Daniel as he hugged them. "You're growing like a weed, Andy. How tall are you now?" Andy didn't know, but after Uncle Daniel talked to them for a minute and Melissa had shown him her braces, they let him take off his hat and coat.

He looked like something between C. S. Lewis (if you've ever seen pictures of him) and Santa Claus. This is an accurate description, because he was an English teacher (like C. S. Lewis) during the school year, and Santa Claus (like Santa Claus) at the mall during the Christmas season. But he had no beard and little hair on his head. He was a big man with a big gut and a big, merry face. His cheeks would redden from the smallest exertion. His eyes were dark and bright at the same time (if you know what I mean), and they had a special quality to them: if you were a good kid and you looked into them, you felt wonderful; if you were bad, they made you feel uncomfortable until you told him what you'd done. And he was always forgiving. Ada had noticed that his eyes had a similar effect on the adults. The good ones liked Uncle Daniel and the mean ones hated him without knowing why.

Uncle Daniel had come bearing gifts, for "spoiling the children," as Ada's grouchy old Grandpa would say. He was one of those people who hated him for no reason, but he was not in the room at the moment, and therefore I don't have to talk about him. Uncle Daniel brought a yoyo out of his suitcase for Andy, a blue yoyo with flashing red lights when you let it unwind. He then pulled a silver dollar out from behind Melissa's ear, which he gave to her (the dollar, not the ear). Finally he brought out books for everyone to read: such wonderful books as *Peter Pan*, *Alice's Adventures in Wonderland*, *The*

Princess and the Goblin, *The Hobbit*, and *The Lion, The Witch and The Wardrobe*. Ada used to like these, before she started reading magazines.

"These are for you too, Ada," Uncle Daniel said as he showed them the books, then added, "I talked to your parents, and I thought you might like this." He handed her the most recent issue of Ada's favorite magazine. I don't know what it was because I don't read them, but Ada certainly knew all about it, and she thanked him.

Then Uncle Daniel put logs in the fireplace. He got his lighter out of his coat pocket and found the lighter fluid, and he started a little crackling fire that made the room much warmer and filled it with a yellow glow.

"Uncle Dan," said Andy, rewinding his yoyo, "You promised to tell us a story when you came."

Just at that moment, I'm sorry to say, Grandpa came into the room. He wore shorts that were far too short and a t-shirt that was far too small. "Still filling their heads with nonsense, Danny?" he said with a sneer. "It's all foolishness. You'll never make them respectable adults like that." The twins drooped their heads as if they were being scolded, and Ada felt uncomfortable. But Uncle Daniel, who was never affected by mean-spirited people, shrugged his shoulders and gave a great, deep laugh. "Who wants to be a respectable adult when we have so much nonsense to talk about? But I think Ada is getting too old for stories by now. Right, Ada?"

"I don't know," said Ada without making eye contact with anyone.

Grandpa soon went downstairs without another word.

After this, Andy and Melissa pleaded excitedly with Uncle Daniel to tell them a story. "Do you want me to read one or make one up?" he said.

"Make one up!" they cried.

"All right then, let's have a go at it," he said, rubbing his hands together. He sat in a chair by the fireplace, and all eyes were on him—except Ada's. She was trying to read her magazine and take no interest in the story, but that didn't last long. In fact, it didn't last longer than the first sentence.

"Have I ever told you," Uncle Daniel began, "about Ada's adventure concerning the window in an unlikely place? Oh, yes, she told me all about it herself. This happened several years ago."

Ada was surprised and amused. She didn't even notice that she'd put down her magazine and was watching Uncle Daniel, listening to his enchanting voice weave a story of magic and wonder. This is the tale he told.

CHAPTER ONE

WHEREIN ADA FINDS
A WINDOW IN AN UNLIKELY PLACE

One autumn day, when Ada was younger, she was walking in a forest. It was a pine forest with a thick layer of soft, prickly, brown needles underfoot. Ada could see far in every direction, because the tall, skinny trees, which looked like they'd been planted in rows, were needleless up to the point where they met the sky and spread a green canopy over the whole wood.

It was late afternoon, and sunbeams peaked through the green ceiling to the forest floor, the light making the reddish-brown forest glow drowsily. And as Ada's feet crunched and shuffled on the cushion of pine needles, she daydreamed. As far as I know, she wasn't thinking about anything in particular, especially not about where she was (for she was pretty confident how to get back) or about her parents' telling her not to stray too far (for she was sure to forget whatever her parents said).

She wandered further and further from the house but pretty much in a straight line. She would have had no trouble finding her way back if something hadn't happened that got her turned around just as she was about to turn back. It was growing dark. Ada sighed, knowing she should return. She was enjoying her solitary walk and wished it didn't have to end so soon, feeling somehow as if she had been expecting something.

Just then there was a bright flash of light. It was as bright as lightning and as soon gone, but there were no dark clouds, no thunder, and no other flash. Ada thought that it must have been either lightning or a camera, but lightning isn't silent, and camera flashes aren't so bright.

Without thinking about getting lost, she started off in the direction from which she judged the light had come. The sky was darkening quickly now, and the trees were silhouetted against the gathering dusk and the distant red sunset. It started to get cold as the first fireflies glowed and the crickets and cicadas began chirping. Still Ada was driven on by curiosity.

While Ada was still a ways off, she saw unmistakably a brighter patch in the forest. It wasn't the faint glow of a bonfire but a solid white beam like a spotlight. Now Ada grew wary. If there were other people in the woods, she wanted to see them before they saw her, in case she needed to run away. She snuck from tree to tree, peeking out from each to see if anyone was there. But there was no one and no sound, and her sneaking slowed her progress.

Stars were visible through the trees as Ada moved closer to the source of the light. As she did so, she noticed two things. First, she smelled a fresh spring-day-like scent on a warm breeze which met her unexpectedly. Second, she heard the whistling of wind.

Then all at once she came around a thick tree and saw a marvelous sight. There was a square hole about the size of a small window in a great tree. Sunlight poured from it to the ground. Ada had to squint as she looked at its brightness. A sudden gust of wind roared out of the hole, and the warm blast blew back her hair.

All the surrounding woods were dark, but from the tree came light and wind and the fresh smell of spring.

Ada was awestruck, rooted to the spot. It gave her time for her eyes to adjust and for her mind to take in what she was seeing.

Finally Ada worked up the courage to approach the window. When she looked in she found a whole world inside! She saw a little man sitting at the edge of a huge white fountain with three tiers and a dazzling column of water shooting up into the air. The fountain was in the center of a well-kept lawn, surrounded by a circle of tall stones standing on end and supporting a giant ring of stones lying on top. Outside the stone circle was a village. There were houses, each carved out of a single rock and complete with windows and doors and chimneys from which the lazy smoke was floating up over the trees. Beyond the village was forest, and in the great distance there were mountains as far as the eye could see.

But what caught her attention right away was the little man. He was sitting on the edge of the ivory pool into which the water of the fountain was falling. He was a short, stocky man—though Ada was not much taller then—with brown boots and brown clothing and a silver belt. He had a dark, pointed beard and earth-colored, leathery skin. The little man was actually a dwarf, as you may have guessed. Ada soon guessed the same, though it was hard to believe. The dwarf was filling a couple of buckets with water from the fountain.

Ada was saved the trouble of deciding what to do next. Out of nowhere a dog jumped up at the window and started barking its head off. Startled, Ada fell back into the darkness and the pine needles, which stung her hands. The dog's head was popping up and down at the window. Ada scrambled to her feet and hid behind the nearest tree. It was just in time, too, because as Ada peeked out, she saw the dwarf come to the window.

She jerked her head back, but when she peeked again, the dwarf didn't appear to have seen her. He was looking to see what the dog was barking at. Finally, the dwarf bent down to pick something up, a squeegee, and wiped the window away with a streak and a squeak. In two swipes the window was gone, the light was gone, and Ada was left in total darkness.

The fear surprised her. For a moment, before her eyes grew accustomed to the darkness, she could see nothing, and she realized that she was lost in the forest. Ada shuddered and grew cold and frightened, and somewhere deep in the dark an owl hooted. Nearly paralyzed by fear, Ada moved toward the windowless tree and ran her fingers across the bark to find the edges, but there was no trace of a window. It was just a tree.

For a few minutes Ada stood still, but doing that only made her colder. So she walked a little way in an attempt to find her way home. But in the end she went back to the tree, slumped down, and started to cry.

I don't know how long she cried or how many times she prayed for help, but I hope she didn't have to wait long. The chilly air gave her goosebumps, and the nighttime noises scared her. She wished that she had listened to her parents now. She wished that she were back in her grandparents' warm cabin with a blanket, a mug of hot cocoa, and her chapstick.

But however long Ada cried (it seemed like an eternity to her), help did come (as it often does), though from a most unlikely place. As Ada wept, the strangest things began to happen. She heard a squeak and saw a beam of light. Then she heard another squeak somewhere else and another light appeared. Then another and another all around her. The squeaking and the light grew and grew. Soon the squeaking stopped, but the light remained. Ada looked up and with teary vision squinted at the light coming from the windows that had appeared in all the surrounding trees. There was a dwarf in each window, and they were all looking at her.

"What's all this racket about?" said one of the dwarves.

CHAPTER TWO

WHEREIN ADA LEAVES
ONE WORLD FOR ANOTHER

Ada sniffed and wiped the tears out of her eyes, struck silent by the dwarf who addressed her so rudely. Luckily another spoke up for her.

"Why don't we help her?" The voice had come from another window, though she couldn't see the speaker's face because it was backlit by the sun of their world. "Why don't we let her in?" the voice said. The dwarves started to debate this amongst themselves.

"Who's that talking?" said the first dwarf. "Is that you, Lithglib? Speak up, if you want to be heard!"

"I SAID WHY DON'T WE LET HER IN!" repeated Lithglib. "She's just a little girl, she's lost, she's scared, and it's the middle of the night in her world."

"Let her in? What nonsense!" replied the first dwarf.

"Why is it nonsense?" persisted Lithglib.

"Because it's never been done before! And we're not about to start now!"

Again the dwarves muttered amongst themselves. They seemed to be in no danger of coming to an agreement. Things might have gone differently for Ada, had not a third dwarf interceded for her. Just then the burly wife of Mr. Backet—that was the first dwarf's name—came up behind him.

There was a struggle. "Dagnabit, she-dwarf! Leave me be!" cried Mr. Backet.

"Out of the way, dear!" sang Mrs. Backet with unshakeable cheerfulness. "Oh, look at the little deary!" she said as soon as she saw Ada. "She's so cold and frightened! Mr. Backet, you brute, how dare you bother this poor thing! Give me your squeegee at once. I'm going to let her in. Oh, look what you've done, you old goat! You spilled all the water. Go and fetch some more from the fountain this instant, or I don't know when you're going to eat supper again!"

The other dwarves laughed. With some words not fit for polite company, Mr. Backet picked up his bucket and went to the fountain to fill it. By this time Ada had stood up, and she could see him. When he returned, the big she-dwarf bent down below the window.

The next thing Ada knew, a light appeared at her feet as another opening into the dwarf world squeaked open. It was big enough for her to crawl through.

"Come on, deary. Don't be shy," said Mrs. Backet with all the sweetness in her power. "What will I say to your mother if you catch a cold?"

Ada hesitated for a moment, but only for a moment. She did not fear them. They were too ordinary and ridiculous for that. So she got down on the cold hard ground, the needles stabbing her hands and knees, and crawled into the tree. One moment she could see her own breath, the next she was wrapped in a blanket of air and light, crawling on grass as soft as her own bed. A welcome warmth met her on the wind of that world.

She hardly had time to savor the moment, however, before she was scooped up by Mrs. Backet and carried away. The other dwarves were in an uproar.

"Welcome to Easelheath," said the dwarf named Lithglib as she was carried by. She had time only to return him a grateful smile, as Mrs. Backet held her in her flabby arms. Lithglib smiled meekly and watched her go. It was strange, but she thought his face was both kind and penitent.

Before she knew it, Ada was carried past the thunderous fountain, between the pillars of the stone circle, and into a stone house. Once inside, she was given hot tea, cookies, and porridge, followed by a stern order from Mrs. Backet to "catch a bit of shuteye," which Ada was happy to obey. After all, she felt quite tired. It was now past her bedtime at home, though it was day in the dwarf world. Adults call this jetlag, though no one I know of has ever gotten it from so short a journey.

At any rate, Ada was led upstairs by Mrs. Backet and shown into a guest room with a soft bed. She fell asleep almost immediately after reading the titles of a few books on the shelf: *A Dwarf-boy's First Book of Smithing*, *The Complete Guide to Precious Stones*, *An Anthology of Gnomic Verse*, and *Magic Rune Engraving for Everybody*.

When Ada awoke, it was to far less pleasant circumstances. She heard the buzz of a mosquito and, without opening her eyes, swatted the air in front of her face. But the buzzing only grew louder, or else she began to realize just how loud it was. What was more, there was an unaccountable wind on her face. It suddenly occurred to her that she was being fanned by large wings.

At that moment, Ada opened her eyes and found, to her amazement, the largest and most hideous mosquito she had ever seen in her life. It was the size of an owl. It was lucky that she saw it when she did, too, because at that moment it decided to strike.

Ada rolled off the bed just as the creature's lance-like proboscis pierced the mattress. What Ada did next deserves praise, for even though she was terrified, she had the presence of mind to throw the blanket over the giant mosquito as it was freeing itself from the bedding. Then she put the heaviest of the aforementioned books in her pillowcase and hefted it to bash the writhing bump in the bed, but it was too late, for the creature had gotten out from under the blanket and rose into the air.

Ada backed up to the other end of the room and stood ready with the pillow in case it attacked again. It did. The creature had apparently spotted her, for it stopped buzzing this way and that and hovered in one spot. Its soulless black eyes unnerved her, but Ada stayed firm, ready. Then it flew straight at her with its long proboscis sticking out of its face like a spear.

At the right moment, Ada swung the pillow with all her might. There was a great thud as the hardcover book inside the pillowcase slammed into the mosquito. The creature whizzed away and hit the opposite wall and slid to the floor. For a moment the buzzing stopped.

Ada was doing quite well for her first battle. Soon the loud buzzing began again, and again Ada's enemy tried to impale her. Thud! Thump!—again the monster hit the pillow, then the wall, and went down. Ada didn't know how much longer she could keep this up. Sooner or later, she would get tired or the creature would get lucky and skewer her.

The monster flew at her a third time. Ada gave it all she had one last time and knocked it straight through the window. With a crash, it broke through the glass and was gone.

Relieved, Ada did the only thing left to do. She promptly fainted.

This time when she awoke, Ada found the concerned face of a dwarf-boy watching over her, though as anyone knows who has fainted before, she didn't at first recognize it as such. First she saw, then she saw a shape, then she saw that it was a person, then that it was a dwarf, and then everything came back to her.

"Are you all right, Miss?" said the beardless dwarf frantically. "I don't mean to barge in on you, but I heard a crash and thought you might need some help—not that I would be the best one to offer it, silly oaf that I am. Do you remember how you passed out?"

"I passed out?" said Ada. The panic in his voice frightened her more than anything else. She wanted him to relax.

"Please, Miss, stay still for a minute more. Stop, please! Don't try to get up." (Ada was unaware that she was trying to sit up.) "If you get up too fast you might faint again. I learned that from my mom. She knows about this kind of thing, and I'm pretty sure that is what she'd say." So Ada stayed still and let the dwarf-boy hover nervously until she was quite sure that she could stand up.

"Did I really faint?" Ada asked once on her feet, still in disbelief. It was not what she had expected. There was no warning. One moment she felt like she was drifting off into a daydream, the next she was lying on her back in a cold sweat.

"Yeah, don't you remember?" he said.

"I didn't know till you told me," she said, adding after a moment, "Please don't tell anyone."

The dwarf seemed reluctant on this point, but nevertheless he promised not to tell. His ears stuck out and his eyes were a little too far apart. He was awkward, but Ada thought he was nice.

"My name is Rowan Backet, but my friends call me Racket. You can call me Racket even if you don't want to be my friend—but, of course, I hope you do. Don't worry about remembering my name. I can just tell it to you again. I—I don't mean that you have a bad memory or anything. What I meant was—" Racket stopped himself and began again. "What's your name, Miss?"

"Ada," she said. "Do you live here?"

"Not in this room, but I do live in this house," said Racket. "It was my mom who brought you from the World Inside the Trees, against my father's wishes. But he's been wrong before. I for one am glad you came. I forgot to bow." He bowed, adding, "Pleased to make your acquaintance, Miss Ada."

Remembering the monster, Ada looked at the window warily, and also a little ashamedly. Racket asked if there was anything, anything at all that he could do for her.

"You must have some big mosquitoes here," said Ada.

"Not bigger than the end of your finger, I wouldn't think," said Racket. "But what do I know? I'm sure they're humungous compared to the ones from your world. You must not be able to see them at all!"

"No, this was gigantic," insisted Ada. "It was bigger than your head."

Racket touched his head. "That big, you say? Again, who am I to contradict you?—but are you quite sure it was that big? Maybe it was just a bad dream."

"It was big enough to break the window," she said.

Racket was puzzled. But he let it drop and they went downstairs, where a feast was being prepared. Mrs. Backet stirred a big, boiling pot that filled the room with steam and the smell of meat and potatoes.

"Well, if the little deary isn't awake," said Mrs.

Backet. "Restful nap? I hope Rowan didn't wake you."

"Would never do it, Mom," said Racket. "She was already awake when I found her. Right, Miss Ada?" said Racket, winking a little too obviously.

"Oh, Ada, what a lovely name!" said Mrs. Backet. Ada loved the smell of Mrs. Backet's cooking. It reminded her of her grandmother's house on Thanksgiving. "Thank you so much for everything," she said, "but I really have to go home now."

"To be sure, very soon," said Mrs. Backet. "No question about it. But how could I look your parents in the face if I let you out of this house with an empty stomach? You will stay for dinner, won't you? It's almost ready now."

"Well, I guess I could stay a little longer," said Ada, her mouth beginning to water.

"Wonderful!" exclaimed Racket. "I better get an extra chair from the living room. We're so glad you're our guest. My best friend Lithglib is coming, too. I better get two extra chairs!" Ada was delighted to hear that Lithglib, the dwarf who had first spoken on her behalf, was coming. Racket went on, "Mom said that Lithglib was the one who invited you to come out of the World Inside the Trees. Between him and me, he's the clever one, but he had an accident today—"

"Almost ready, Rowan," said Mrs. Backet. "Hurry up with those chairs, and wake your father in the den to tell him dinner's ready, and get the door, dear, that must be Lithglib now."

"I'll tell you about Lithglib's accident later," said Racket over his shoulder on his way to the front door. "Or maybe he'll tell you himself!"

CHAPTER THREE

WHEREIN A TERRIBLE
DISCOVERY IS MADE

Mrs. Backet had indeed prepared a feast. There was steak, fish, chicken, and eggs. There was warm homemade bread with butter and honey. There was stuffing and mashed potatoes and peanuts and chocolate and strawberries, and dates and figs. But, strangely, the best part of all was the water, if it could be called water, for it was remarkably sweet. It was like nothing Ada ever had before. It sparkled in the glass with a starry light of its own. Its sweetness was not like the sweetness of sugar, which can be too sweet. The sweetness of this water could never be too sweet.

This (Ada would soon come to find out) was the living water of the fountain, one of the magical properties of which we have already seen. With it the dwarves opened windows between the two worlds. When Ada drank it, she was completely refreshed, like a young plant opening its leaves to receive the air and the sun. It made her feel like singing, or perhaps it was the water singing inside her. All at once she felt happy and sad, young and old, humble and of great worth. She remembered disobeying her parents and thought about how worried they must be, and she was sorry. She remembered praying that someone would find her in the darkness, and she was grateful. She looked at her dinner companions to see if the water had the same effect on them.

"Thank you for dinner, Mrs. Backet," said Lithglib politely, looking a little glum and distracted. He took a sip of his water, and it seemed to raise his spirits.

"Thank you, dear," said Mrs. Backet, beaming. "Just some things I found in the cupboards." The water didn't have any noticeable effect on the Backets, most likely because it was not possible for Racket and Mrs. Backet to get any livelier, and because Mr. Backet was just impossible. The latter halfheartedly mumbled his thanks and hardly looked up from his food.

"Yes, thank you, Mrs. Backet!" said Ada, a jolly sight more cheerful than before. "Where does this water come from?"

"Bless me!" exclaimed Mrs. Backet. "I forget you're not from around here, deary." She took a breath, and Racket seized upon this opportunity to answer.

"It comes from the Fountain," said he. "We call it living water. It is the reason we all live in Easelheath. It gives us good health, and it's the sweetest water in the world. The spring that feeds the Fountain comes from the Calix, which is a magic cup that forever overflows and protects our village from evil, and—"

"Breathe, Racket," said Lithglib wryly. He and Ada shared a smile.

"What is the Calix?" asked Ada, for Racket had spoken too quickly for her. She saw Lithglib look away in shame when she asked this question and wondered what was the matter.

"The Calix is a magic cup," said Racket, happy to be invited to speak again, "It is always overflowing. It's the source of the Fountain. It stands on top of a rock in the middle of the Calix Pond, where Lithglib got in trouble for fishing and almost drowned this morning—sorry, Lithglib, did you want to tell her?" (Lithglib's countenance sunk lower, and Ada pitied him.) "Anyway, the Calix protects Easelheath from monsters or something—"

"Confound it, boy!" Mr. Backet exploded. "Don't you ever stop talking! While you're at it, why don't you tell her all the village secrets and give her the keys to all the houses, so she can come back with whatever gang of gypsies left her behind and cut our throats in the middle of the night!"

"Shame on you, Mr. Backet!" said his wife. "That's no way to talk around company!" With that, Mrs. Backet cried and absolutely would not be consoled until he had apologized, which he did gruffly. Ada was feeling rather low now, too. Nobody wants to be spoken ill of for no reason, and some rather cruel persons would do well to remember that.

At any rate it all settled down soon, and Racket and his mother were back to their cheerful selves again. Only Lithglib seemed not to have cheered up. Ada wanted him to drink more of his water. Racket, on the other hand, didn't need encouragement. He lifted his glass and drained it in one drink. His mother scolded him, but it was too late.

"So tell us about your accident, Lithglib!" He could not restrain himself any longer. "Tell us about how you almost drowned fishing in Calix Pond, and how Hyke jumped in and saved you!" Here he turned to Ada and said, "Hyke is Lithglib's dad. Well, sort of. Lithglib's adopted. Tell us about your accident, Lithglib!"

Lithglib sighed, or rather deflated. And seeing that Racket would not be pacified until Lithglib told his tale, which obviously caused him pain, he began.

"I was fishing—in Calix Pond."

Mr. Backet grumbled something about what he would have done to him if he were his boy. Mrs. Backet shushed him, and Lithglib continued penitently.

"Like a fool, I was standing up in my boat and casting my line in the direction of the Calix. I must have caught the lip of the cup with my hook, because the next thing I remember was a bright flash of light and then I was in the water."

"Ruddy lucky you didn't break it," growled Mr. Backet. He was shushed again, though he had already finished, by Mrs. Backet, who listened to Lithglib silently with tears in her eyes. Ada was close to tears herself in spite of the living water.

Lithglib accepted Mr. Backet's rebuke without objection and continued: "Hyke found me in time and saved me. I woke up in my own bed."

"I saw the flash," said Racket, still heedless of his friend's grief, "I thought it was lightning, but then there was no thunder."

"Me too," said Ada aloud. She couldn't help it. It had just occurred to her that this is what she had seen.

"You too, Miss Ada?" said Racket, puzzled. "I thought you were still in the tree-world when that happened, if you'll forgive my manner of speaking. I didn't mean to challenge you."

"Somebody left a window open. The light must have come through it," said Ada, for she might as well talk about it now, though she felt sorry for Lithglib's sake. However, something still confused her. "But that can't be, because I saw Lithglib only a little while afterwards."

Lithglib sat pensively for a moment. "Time must be different here. A few minutes in your world must be several hours in ours. That means that you'll probably get back to your world about the same time you left."

The ramifications of this were just beginning to dawn on her—it would still be the middle of the night in the forest when she returned—when something happened that upset everyone's reflections. There was a scream outside, followed by the sound of general panic and uproar.

Mrs. Backet ran to the window, turned pale, and said to her husband, "Mr. Backet, you'd better go outside." He did so, and the three children ran to the door to see what all the hubbub was about. Ada was only a little taller than the dwarf boys and had no trouble seeing from behind them. This is what she saw.

All the dwarves of the village were gathered around the fountain, shouting and making quite a commotion. It was not obvious to her at first why they were so upset, until Lithglib said,

"What have I done! The water!"

Then she saw it. The fountain had dried up.

"I must have broken it!" he cried. "The Calix! This is all my fault!"

Ada's heart broke for him. He was sure to be in a lot of trouble now (she didn't know the half of it). At the same time she was conscious of the fact that the dwarves now had a lot bigger concerns than a lost human girl, and so she resolved to return to her own world and face her troubles on her own.

"I'm so sorry, Lithglib. You seem so nice." She didn't know what to say. "I should probably go home now."

Lithglib turned to her, and she could see that a fresh pang of guilt overspread his face. "I'm so sorry, Ada," he said. "I've trapped you here!"

"What?" she said with some alarm.

"Don't you understand?" said Lithglib. "Without the Calix, there is no more living water. Without the water, the squeegees don't work. Without the squeegees, we can't make windows. And without the windows—you can never go home!"

CHAPTER FOUR

WHEREIN THE DWARVES
SEE THEIR PREDICAMENT

"But there's still some living water left, isn't there?" said Ada. Indeed there was. Ada and Lithglib carefully retrieved their glasses from the table. The light had gone out of them. This didn't bode well, but they refused to give up hope. Lithglib had hardly touched his, and he poured the rest of Ada's water into his own glass and told Racket to fetch a squeegee. This command was speedily obeyed.

And despite Mrs. Backet's protestations, the three children set out at once towards the very tree by which Ada had entered Easelheath, careful not to spill a drop or to get too close to the growing riot around the Fountain. The light was failing, but that is not a problem for the eyes of dwarves, which were made to work best in dark, underground places. They identified Ada's tree without trouble.

"Sorry to see you go so soon, Miss Ada," said Racket with feeling. "Do come again."

"I'll try," said Ada sincerely.

"I'm sorry for the trouble I've caused you," said Lithglib, wetting the squeegee with the water from his cup. "Please don't think ill of the dwarves on my account."

"Never," she replied. She wanted to hug him, but she didn't want him to spill what might be the last of the dwarves' magic water.

Lithglib then raised the squeegee to the tree, paused for a moment, and raked it down the bark. There was no effect.

"No!" he cried, pouring out the rest of the water on the squeegee, then immediately swiping the tree with it. Nothing happened. He did it again and again, harder and faster, but apart from scrapping off a good deal of bark, he could do nothing. Ada realized now that she was stuck here. Racket was crying and Lithglib was working himself into a frenzy. Ada calmly put her hand on Lithglib's shoulder. Feeling her touch, he stopped scarring the tree, let his arms fall to his sides, drooped his head, and let the squeegee fall to the ground. He could not look at her, and she thought he might be crying.

"It's all right, Lithglib," she said. "It's not your fault." By which she meant, of course, that she didn't blame him, since in fact it probably was his fault. Finally, the three of them walked back to the house to await the result of it all. Mrs. Backet wept buckets for Ada and rambled about not knowing what she would say to her parents. Ada wept too, but not for herself. Lithglib could not sink any lower. Racket, overcome by the emotions of everyone around him, cried no less than anyone else. A shadow fell over Lithglib, if not the world.

There was still water left in the house, though when Ada tasted it, it tasted like plain old water from back home, maybe a little stale now. The four of them sat without speaking at the kitchen table and waited for Mr. Backet to return. The noise outside grew quieter and eventually the crowd began to disperse. They now began speaking in whispers. Lithglib gave Ada to understand that he fully expected the mob to drag him from the house at any moment, and when it didn't happen he said that his crime must not yet be general knowledge.

"Tomorrow I will have to confess my crime to Easelheath," he said gloomily. Ada didn't know what to say, so she simply put her hand on his. It was cold and his dwarvish skin was tough. At last, when the darkness outside was impenetrable to Ada's eyes, Mr. Backet returned. Accompanying him was another dwarf who Ada soon realized was Lithglib's adoptive father. His name was Hyke. Mr. Backet glared at Lithglib but said not a word. If Ada was expecting Hyke to be angry with his son, she was much mistaken. She saw nothing but kindness and sympathy in his features. In fact, his presence seemed to have a calming effect on the whole room. He was bigger and stronger than Mr. Backet and looked more like a woodsman, more rustic than any of the dwarves whom Ada had met. He came and put his hand on his son's back, saying in a gentle way, "Come, son. We must talk." Lithglib followed his father into another room without lifting his eyes from the floor. The door closed behind him.

"That boy has a lot to answer for in the morning," growled Mr. Backet. This was too much for his family to handle. Mrs. Backet burst into fresh sobs and Racket ran upstairs to his room. Ada followed him. Her concern for her own troubles was nothing compared to her concern for Lithglib and the dwarves. She had a big heart. She still does.

She found Racket crying, lying face down on his bed. She sat in a chair beside him.

"I'm sorry, Ada," he said. "I'm sorry for everything."

"It's okay, Racket," she said in the calming tone she

learned from her mother.

"But it's not okay—if you'll forgive me. I didn't mean to challenge you. It's just that I'm afraid for all of us. Lithglib is going to be in a lot of trouble. We're all in a lot of trouble. Without the Calix, Easelheath won't last long. Monsters will come." Ada tried to hide a shudder, remembering the giant mosquito from earlier, no doubt the first of many to come. Ada made sure the door to the room with the broken window was closed fast. Hyke and Lithglib stayed with the Backets that night. It is doubtful that anyone slept.

The next morning a general assembly was called. All of Easelheath was required to attend, though the mandate was unnecessary. Nothing could have kept the citizens away. After a brief and wordless breakfast, Hyke, Lithglib, Ada, and the Backets left the house in solemn procession and headed towards a huge house on the hill, which according to Racket belonged to one of the village elders. Mr. Backet double and triple locked the front door behind them, although the only thing that could break into a dwarf's house is another dwarf, and all of those were in the same place. The Backets (and company) were almost the last ones on the road. Lithglib looked like he was going to his death, and Ada tried in vain to comfort him. The sky was gray, and the wind was dead. There was a light rain. The party plodded along the main road, a dirt road packed down by years of dwarvish feet, past the boulder-houses which seemed so happy to Ada the day before, and past the uncanny silence of the Fountain and the stone circle, which now seemed to take on a dark and foreboding aspect, like something out of a horror film. She grew afraid of the shadows, fearing they hid evil and creeping things. If mosquitoes could grow so large, how big would spiders, bats, and snakes get? She tried not to think about it and consequently thought of nothing else until they reached the front gate of the elder's mansion.

The mansion had been cut out of stone. In fact, most of it was underground deep inside the cliff face. The entrance and front part of the house was merely a giant façade elaborately carved into the rock, made to look like so many windows and pillars. Ada failed to mention that she was afraid both of the dark and of close spaces, not that it would have done any good. Luckily for her, at the front door each of the adults took a torch from a golden bowl of fire supported by a golden tripod and set out for this purpose.

They plunged into the darkness and walked two abreast down, down, down a long corridor. The steps were perfectly symmetrical and of equal height. Along the walls there hung the most intricate breastplates, helmets, shields, axes, and hammers, made with silver and gold, studded with gems of every description, and inscribed with finely wrought runes. Dwarves' work. Ada had never seen anything like it, although she was not in the right mood to appreciate it.

The noise increased as they descended, until at last the passageway opened up into a huge underground stadium or theater. Although Ada's human eyes could have wished for more light, she could see grades of stone benches separated by aisles leading all the way down to the stage. The meeting had not yet been called to order, and the elders on the stage and the citizens in the audience were talking animatedly amongst themselves. The adults deposited their torches in a stand and the whole party took their seats.

CHAPTER FIVE

WHEREIN LITHGLIB IS
SENTENCED TO EXILE

No sooner had the party sat down than the chief elder of the dwarves banged his hammer on a gavel to call the assembly to order. It took some doing, but finally the citizens of Easelheath were quieted.

"You all know the reason for this meeting," he began in a loud voice which reverberated through the underground cavern. "The Fountain has run dry, the spell of the Calix has been broken, and Easelheath is now in desperate straits." The crowd roared in agreement. Individual dwarves started shouting out fearsome reports. One claimed that his fields had been burned by firebats, another that gremlins and goblins had been seen in the mines, a third that the lake had turned to acid and killed the fish. Several claimed to have been attacked by insects of unusual size, and Ada could attest at least to that. The chief elder banged on his gavel again, but to no effect. The crowd did not fall silent until he produced the Calix. He held it up so that all could see it. There were gasps and mutterings, then silence. It was a silver chalice with sapphires set in runes running around the circumference of the rim. One of the sapphires had shattered.

"As you can see, the Calix no longer flows. Our best smiths have worked on the cup throughout the night to no avail. The magic, once lost, is lost forever. And lacking the art of our ancestors, we have not the skill to make another chalice. Two things are left for us to do. First, we must put on the ancient armor of our fathers, arm ourselves, and dig deep into the mountain, where we have ever been strongest and best fortified. There, let any enemies who dare come and attack us. We shall sell our lives dearly, as we have ever done. As for the second matter before us, let the guilty dwarf come forward and be brought to justice for his crime!" There was a general uproar of agreement.

Ada looked at Lithglib. At first he was paralyzed by fear and the heaviness of what he was about to do. Then Hyke put his hand on his back and whispered some encouraging words in his ear. Hyke was strong for his son, and some of that strength seemed to flow into Lithglib. For after a few more moments of dread, Lithglib rose from his seat, moved to the aisle and started walking down towards the stage. The audience fell silent upon seeing him. They had not expected the culprit to be a child, for so the dwarves considered him, since he had no beard. (Dwarves do not get their beards until they are about thirty years old.) Perhaps they were a little ashamed of themselves now, but if so, it didn't last long.

Lithglib, having reached the bottom, climbed up the side steps to the stage, walked wearily across it in full view of all the citizens of Easelheath, and came to the golden podium, which the chief elder, not without amazement, yielded to him. Ada's heart was pounding. Lithglib stood there for a few moments, working up the courage to speak. At last he lifted his eyes to the audience, turned a little pale, and made a few false starts before he began his confession—his voice cracking, his speech halting.

"I—It's my fault," he said, almost inaudibly. Then raising his voice, he said again, "It's my fault. I broke the Calix with my fishing hook. I was fishing in Calix Pond, which is against the law. I take full responsibility. I'm sorry. I deserve whatever punishment you decide. I won't complain." Once more the dwarves erupted in debate. For many, the trouble he had caused outweighed their pity. Others argued that death, which was the lawful penalty for touching the Calix, though there had never been an occasion for it before, was too severe a punishment for a child. They said banishment was more just. A minority said he should receive no official punishment at all on account of his youth, but when they realized there was no hope of his getting off scot-free, they threw in their lot with the exile crowd, since they needed help against the death crowd, who maintained that he should be tried as an adult, beard or no beard. Ada prayed for exile, since it was growing more and more obvious that that would be the best possible outcome in the present case. Mrs. Backet and her son could not bear to look. Lithglib awaited his fate with resignation. He had not the least hope for himself. Hyke's features were stern and inscrutable, as though he had been turned to stone.

At last the chief elder called the assembly to order again and told the crowd that he would deliberate with the elders. He went up to the bench, like a judge's bench, and spoke with the committee of elders who sat there. After a short time, shorter than Ada would have liked, the chief elder came back and took the podium from Lithglib, having him stand off to the side for judgment.

He said, "It is the judgment of this council, Lithglib, son of Hyke, that for the crimes of trespassing upon the sacred pond and destroying the Calix, you shall be forever banished from Easelheath, effective two days hence; after which time, if you are found anywhere in Easelheath, you will be arrested and summarily executed. Be gone within two days and never return, upon pain of death!"

It is impossible to describe how Ada felt at this moment, watching her new friend bear the judgment of the whole village. She wept for him. The crowd was more or less pleased with the result but soon put it out of their minds. They had bigger problems to deal with now.

Lithglib was led off the stage with an armed escort, lest someone try to hurt him. This prevented Ada and the rest of the party from seeing him until they got outside. They had been inside less than an hour, but when they came to the surface, the world had grown perceptibly darker and wilder. The raindrops were larger and heavier, still not enough to drench their bodies, but quite enough to dampen their mood. There was an armed guard ready to escort the villagers back to Easelheath, dwarves in ancient, shining armor, wielding swords and battleaxes as tall as their owners, their armor dulled only by the general gloom that had fallen over the land. The party was joined by Lithglib as they walked down the road, everyone on the alert. The trees drooped, and their branches sagged under the weight of the rain. The birdsong was no more. In its place was the cawing of crows and less natural sounds coming from the throats of birds and animals Ada had never heard before. There were eyes in the woods watching the dwarves pass along the road. Ada could feel them growing bolder. She stayed close to Lithglib and Hyke.

"Mr. Hyke," said Ada, looking up at him, "there

are—things—watching us from the woods."

"I know," he said. "I see them. Don't you worry. They won't attack us just yet."

Ada could have done without the "just yet," but nevertheless she felt that nothing could hurt her as long as Hyke was close. It was the same feeling she had when her dad was home. How she wished he were here!

Then the mosquitoes came. They were bigger than the one Ada had fought. These were the size of vultures! At first they just flew over the crowd. A section of the foot traffic shouted and ducked each time one flew overhead. They were not yet low enough for the soldiers to deal with them. Ada felt the wind of wings on the back of her neck as one buzzed over them from behind. The women screamed, and everyone crouched as they walked, everyone except Hyke. He picked up several stones the size of golf balls and took a sling from his pocket, then, walking a little off to the right, he loaded his sling and started swinging it round and round. It whistled with every revolution. When the flying monster returned, Hyke was ready for it. He swung the sling faster, the pitch of its whistling rose, and with a final spin he slung the rock straight at the oncoming creature, hitting it dead center and killing it instantly. It fell from the sky and landed in the gutter. The crowd cheered. In this way Hyke took down six of the giant mosquitoes. He was not alone, for the insects started to attack the crowd. The soldiers bashed the ones coming from the sides with their shields and then crushed them with their war-hammers and axes once they were down. There were also a few bows among the citizens, and more than one monstrous insect was brought down by arrows. Nevertheless, a few got through and pierced citizens with their lances. This caused a general panic, and soon the villagers were routed. They ran madly down the hill, and in the end more were injured from being trampled than being impaled. Ada and her friends, not without some bumps and bruises of their own, arrived at the Backets' house out of breath and panting. It was then that Ada noticed Hyke wasn't with them. This caused her some alarm, until Lithglib, in answer to her look, told her that he had left and said that he would meet them at the Backets' later.

Once inside, they immediately set to work fortifying the house, which, since it was made out of stone, could only be entered by the front door, the windows, or the trap door in the living room floor. This trap door, Ada learned, led to the tunnels underground which connected all of Easelheath and would certainly now be used to get around instead of the front door. Mr. Backet and the boys set to work repairing the window in the guest room—they were now ready to believe Ada's story—and nailing boards over all the windows, leaving only the smallest cracks to peek out of.

When Ada did peek out, she saw no one outside, just the insects flying over the rooftops and landing on the sides of houses. Once she saw a huge, hairy boar the size of a bull with four tusks coming out of its mouth sniffing around the village. The beast frightened her, but soon she pitied him. The insects found him. First one, then another mosquito landed on his back and plunged their face-spears into him and started to drain his blood. The boar squealed and started to run, but they swarmed him until she could hardly see him for all the mosquitoes on him. He did not make it more than twenty feet towards the woods before he went down for good. They made short work of him. Ada turned away sick to her stomach. Afterwards she resolved not to look outside.

There was not much light in the house since the windows were covered, so (probably for her sake) the dwarves lit some lamps and hung them in the rooms and halls. They all sat in the living room listening to the buzzing outside. Everyone's nerves were on edge. Ada sat between Racket and Lithglib. Everyone was looking at the trap door in the floor, and though no one said so, Ada knew that they were all waiting for Hyke to return.

CHAPTER SIX

WHEREIN LITHGLIB IS JOINED BY FRIENDS

When hours passed and still there was no sign of Hyke, Ada began to worry that something had happened to him, although if anyone could take care of himself, surely he could. Mr. Backet by this time had armed himself. The ancestral armor of his family, the heirlooms of the Backets, came down off the walls of his den. Mrs. Backet helped him into it as the children watched. He looked stalwart and formidable in his war-gear. Pride and respect stirred in their hearts. His disagreeable nature was forgotten as he stood like an ancient sentinel in the doorway between the kitchen and the living room resting his hands on his battleaxe.

Mrs. Backet and the children were back in the living room waiting for Hyke. Not a moment too soon there was a hard knock on the trap door that made Ada jump. There were three knocks, then two, then four slow ones. Mr. Backet came to life, walked over, kneeled, took hold of the iron ring in the floor, and lifted the trap door. Hyke's head appeared and then the rest of him, carrying a large leather pack. He too was wearing armor, splendidly wrought, and a hammer with a long handle on his back. When he stood in the room, thus arrayed, he looked like a titan. Ada was surprised he fit through the trap door, though it was wide. What he (like all dwarves) lacked in height, he more than made up for in breadth.

"Things are only going to get worse in Easelheath from now on," he said. "It will be safest for you, son, if you leave now by the tunnels. I've packed your gear."

"Aren't you coming with me?" said Lithglib.

"I must stay here and protect the village. As soon as things quiet down here, I shall try to slip away and join you."

"I'm going with Lithglib!" blurted out Racket unexpectedly.

"Me too!" cried Ada more unexpectedly, especially to herself.

"Don't be ridiculous, boy," said Mr. Backet.

"I won't hear of it, children!" cried Mrs. Backet. "My poor nerves couldn't take it! To lose one child is bad enough. To lose three..." The onset of tears prevented her from completing this sentence.

Hyke said nothing. He neither encouraged nor discouraged their resolution, but simply awaited the result of the debate.

"I'm the same age as Lithglib," said Racket to his parents with more courage than anyone thought him capable of. "Where he goes, I go!"

"Me too!" Ada repeated simply, for lack of anything better to say.

"And how will you survive?" said Mrs. Backet, more upset than anything else. "How will you defend yourselves? How will you eat?"

"How will Lithglib do any better without us?" retorted her son.

"Lithglib has made his own bed, and now he has to sleep in it," said Mr. Backet sternly. "There's no sense in you running off to your death with him."

"I've never had much sense, father, as you've always told me. I'm not clever. Anyone can see that. And I don't have much courage, either, except maybe I've got a bit more right now than I'm used to. But what I do have is friends, and though I might not be much use to them, I'm a lot less use to anyone else. What I'm trying to say is—you've always told me to have more backbone. Well, this is me having backbone. I've got two good friends right here, and I mean to keep them. I mean to keep them longer than I keep myself. What I mean to say is—if I can do no better than throw this useless body of mine between my friends and a giant bug, I mean to do it, and do it with a smile."

The vehemence and earnestness of Racket's speech took his parents off guard. Ada wanted to kiss his cheek. Instead she stood there resolutely beside Lithglib and, riding the wave of Racket's courage, said, "I'm going too. Thank you very much, Mr. and Mrs. Backet for all you've done for me, but I'm not a dwarf and I can't go home and I'd rather go with my friends than stay here and wait to get eaten by something."

Mrs. Backet was about to speak again, when Mr. Backet said, rather unexpectedly, "If this is your decision, boy, and you're dwarf enough to back up your words with deeds, then I won't stop you. As for the dryad"—It was a common error among dwarves that humans were tree-spirits, since their only contact with them was through trees—"As for the dryad, she is not our kind, so I won't tell her yea or nay. If she wants to stray from her tree, let her."

"Mr. Backet!" cried his wife, shocked and amazed. She was powerless, and despite all her tears and protestations, the decision had been made.

Racket and Ada cheered. Hyke smiled. "I thought this might happen," he said. He went down the ladder and came back up with two more packs, one the same size as Lithglib's, and a much smaller one for Ada.

Lithglib didn't know what to say. "You don't have to do this, you know," he said with feeling to his friends. "It's my fault. I should suffer this alone." But Racket and Ada wouldn't hear of it. Such is the fierce loyalty of children. They had no thought for the future, only for their friend.

"Open your packs," said Hyke. The children obeyed. The first thing each pulled out was a forest-green cloak with a hood. Hers felt like silk in Ada's fingers, though slightly less bendable and much stronger.

"If you turn it inside out," instructed Hyke, "the cloak is white." Indeed it was. As Ada turned her cloak inside out, she found that it was as white as the driven snow. "That is so that you can hide both in winter and in summer."

"What kind of cloth is this?" asked Ada, still rubbing the silky, thin cloak between her fingers.

"It isn't cloth at all," he answered. "It's metal."

Metal!

"These cloaks are made of silverspun metalweave, lighter than silk and stronger than steel. No blade can pierce them, although you'll still feel it if you get hit with one. They will never rust nor tarnish. Not only that, they hold the fires in which they were made: they will keep you warm through tempest, blizzard, and squall. Each of these took over a century to make. Don't lose them!"

"Where did you get them?" inquired Lithglib.

Hyke smiled again. "They're gifts from the elders, but don't tell anyone. No one is supposed to know. But that's not all they've given you."

Next Lithglib and Racket each pulled out a sheathed sword, about two feet long. Lithglib's sheath was auburn-colored with gold filigree in the shape of a dragon. Racket's was gold with silver filigree and diamonds. Being boys—and boyness is the same everywhere, even across worlds—they immediately drew their swords. Ada took a step back. Each of the broad, two-edged swords had runes engraved in the blades. When the light caught them just right, the runes in Lithglib's blade shone red, in Racket's, blue.

"The runes are the names of your swords," said Hyke. "Lithglib, yours is called Naegling. Rowan, yours is Hrunting."

Racket eyed the runes in his sword with something approaching religious awe. "What do they do!" he cried.

"They cut things," said Hyke good-humoredly. "They won't break or grow dull, but they don't shoot lightning bolts, if that's what you mean."

There was no sword for Ada, but she pulled out several other things just her size. The first was a little dagger, about four inches long, with a silver handle and sheath which, when together, featured a little dwarf cutting stone with a pickaxe in sapphire-blue filigree. It was very pretty. Next there was a little sling and a small blue bag of perfectly smooth stones. Last of all there was a silver locket in the shape of the moon. It was a crescent of silver partially covering a round glass lens, through which Hyke said she could see in the dark.

"But that's not all it does," said he. "Put it on. Now do you see the tiny button on the side? Slide it down until the silver covers the whole lens and the moon is full. And—try not to be alarmed."

She wouldn't have been alarmed if he hadn't said that, but nevertheless she did as he said. She slid the little button slowly downwards, and as she did so a thin silver panel between the crescent and the lens covered the lens completely and completed the circle of the moon. The moment she did so, she heard the briefest noise like a split second of the roar of a waterfall, and then she could no longer see herself. All the dwarves except Hyke nearly jumped out of their skins.

"Where did she go!" they cried.

"She's still there," said Hyke. "Say something, Ada."

"Am I invisible!" she cried with astonishment.

"Almost," said Hyke. "Get up and walk around."

When she did so, you could just barely make out her shape, and only if you were in the same room with her. She looked like she was made out of water or glass. It was rather disorienting to walk like that because she could not see her feet.

Hyke continued: "In darkness or moonlight, you are totally invisible. In sunlight or up close, unless you remain perfectly still, you are nearly invisible. This treasure is Diana's Locket, but it was not made by dwarves."

She slid the locket open again, heard the sound, and reappeared. Lithglib, Racket, and his mother were startled again, even though they were expecting it this time. They gasped and then applauded.

"Who made it?" asked Ada.

"No one knows," said Hyke. "It was found by the dwarves, though not made by them. I was told that it may have come from your world."

"My world? But there's no magic in my world."

"Is there not? Have you not heard of such things

there?"

"We have, but only in stories written a long time ago. I thought they were just stories."

Hyke thought for a moment, then said, "Just because there is no longer magic in your world doesn't mean there never was. The need may have been greater in times past. Or it may still be going on, but your people have blinded themselves to it, which sometimes happens when people turn their backs on their gods."

Ada didn't know what to make of all this, and frankly she was still too overcome with the power of her locket to listen. She wondered if she would be able to keep it after the adventure was over, and whether it would work the same in her own world, if she ever got back. But somehow the thought made her feel guilty. Something inside her told her that such things were only to be used as tools, not for selfish reasons.

All the food and camping gear and other necessities— that is, all the heavy stuff—was in the boys' packs, since dwarves (like ants) are made to carry more than their own body weight, and since dwarves (like men in former times) lived by a strict code of chivalry, or in other words, by the principle of "ladies first," the modern and much diminished form of the old idea.

"There is one thing left," said Hyke, pulling out an object wrapped in white cloth and handing it to Lithglib, who immediately unwrapped it.

"The Calix!" he exclaimed. He was not alone in his exclamations. The silver cup, even in its present state, was not without luster. One could still see one's reflection in it. Its sapphires glittered. "Why would they give me this?"

"Well, they can't fix it, and you can't break it any more. There just might be a way to fix it. Unless you have other plans once you leave Easelheath"—Lithglib owned that he had none—"You might as well journey east and talk to the Sage that lives on Mt. Heofon. He'll know, if anyone does, what is to be done."

CHAPTER SEVEN

WHEREIN THE CHILDREN
SET OUT ON THEIR QUEST

The children felt a lot better now that they had been given the elders' gifts and had someplace to go and something to do. They put on their green cloaks and fastened them with silver brooches shaped like anvils. Ada wore Diana's Locket around her neck and her dagger on her belt. She put the sling and a few stones in her pocket. (Hopefully she would have time to practice with it before she needed it.) The rest she put back in her pack, now mostly empty, and stowed it in Racket's much bigger pack. He didn't mind.

The three children and Hyke stood around the open trap door in the Backets' living room. Mrs. Backet wept copiously and nearly hugged the children to death. Racket and his father awkwardly shook hands. Mr. Backet, in what he probably considered a moment of weakness, wanted to do more, but didn't know how. After a heartfelt round of goodbyes, they climbed down the ladder, first Hyke, then Lithglib, then Ada, then Racket.

Ada instinctively held her locket as she descended into the dark. Then, remembering what it was for, she held it up to her eye and looked through the lens. From pitch-black the tunnel suddenly seemed bathed in pale blue light, as if there were a full moon behind her. She could see from one end of the tunnel to the other. She closed her other eye and walked behind Lithglib and fancied she saw just as well as the dwarves, if not better, though without much depth perception or peripheral vision.

Hyke led them silently down the long, cold, dripping passageway, supported at regular intervals by wooden beams. There were puddles on the ground and wet roots that hung down from the ceiling. Ada tried to avoid these as best she could, and pulled her hood up and held her cloak shut with her free hand. Doing so made her feel warm all over, just as Hyke said. It was like an electric blanket. Now all she needed was hot cocoa and chapstick.

There were tunnels leading off to the right and the left, down many of which Ada saw ladders, no doubt leading to trap doors in the floors of other dwarves' houses. When they got to the end of the tunnel, they came to a T-junction. Hyke turned right, and after a little while longer there was a fork in the passageway, and he took a left. Several turns later Ada hoped that she was not supposed to be memorizing the route. She would never be able to find her way back on her own. But on second thought, they were never allowed to return, so it didn't really matter.

Ada had a nasty thought. What if gigantic snakes started burrowing their way into the tunnel and chasing them? Luckily that didn't happen, although every time some dirt or rocks fell off the walls, she started.

They must have walked several miles underground before they came out and saw the sky again, which was still dreary and colorless, even when she wasn't looking through the locket. The light, such as it was, made Ada's head hurt, and she squinted and blinked. She was still terribly jetlagged and had not slept at all the night before, though she had lain down and closed her eyes for a few hours.

The four came out of a little cave on a slope of tall grass and scattered rocks leading down to the lake. They were now beyond the eastern boundary of Easelheath. The lake had a strong smell which it never had before, said the dwarves. There were dead fish floating on the surface and lying on the beach. They would have to find somewhere else to fill their water skins.

"Here I must leave you," said Hyke, sooner than anyone expected, and much sooner than anyone wished.

"Can't you come with us?" repeated Lithglib, visibly hurt. "We need you more than they do."

"You need me less than you think," said Hyke. "As I said, I shall come after you as soon as things quiet down here. You'll find that the world, with some exceptions, grows less dangerous but more strange the further east you go. Seek the Sage on Mt. Heofon. Good luck to you." With that he disappeared back into the cave, and the three children were alone.

"Things will never quiet down here, not after what I've done," said Lithglib in self-reproach.

"Don't worry, Lithglib," said Racket, "We're with you all the way."

Ada felt her locket as they stood there. It was a comfort to her, knowing that she could disappear at the first sign of danger. She fell into the habit of holding it whenever she didn't feel quite safe, which she had done as soon as Hyke left. She noticed that the boys had rested their hands on their sword hilts about the same time.

With a deep sigh, Lithglib took the lead. All three pulled their cloaks a little closer—the clouds were still dripping halfheartedly—and started to pick their way down the hill between stones, careful not to let their feet get carried away by the steepness of the slope. No use getting a sprained ankle on the first step out the door (so to speak). Their marching order was Lithglib, Ada, then Racket, so that Ada might have one defender in front of her and one behind, an arrangement which made everyone more comfortable.

"I don't mean to whine," said she, picking her steps carefully, "but I'm really tired, Lithglib. Do we have to walk all day?"

"No, we don't," said he. "We've all had a rough night, and we're not in any hurry. Even if the Sage can fix the Calix, we can't do any more harm by losing a few hours."

They avoided the lake as much as possible, the stench of which grew more intolerable the closer they got, and skirted the beach to the left at the bottom of the hill, until, climbing up a short but steep embankment with the aid of tree roots, they gained the road and struck a path due east. The trees on either side of the road joined high overhead and strained out most of what little light came down from the gray afternoon sky, leaving the road dark and threatening. Ada's locket did little to alleviate the gloom and nothing to alleviate the mood. At least there were no giant insects to deal with, not yet anyway.

Racket was unusually quiet. He was obviously out of his element, uncomfortable in the strange new surroundings, and suffering from the same sleep deprivation as the others. He let out a long yawn as he followed behind, then shook his head and opened his eyes wide to try to fight off fatigue. Ada's eyes were heavy, and she would certainly fall asleep if she stopped walking. Only Lithglib seemed not to grow weary, driven on perhaps by his guilt.

The children walked along in silence for a long way and met no one on the road. Everyone who lived around here lived in Easelheath, and everyone in Easelheath was buttoned away inside their homes. It was unlikely that they would stir from them, and then only to go underground.

"As soon as things get bad enough," said Lithglib. "All the villagers will retreat into the chief elder's mansion, and then further and further underground. That is the way of dwarves." Ada wondered if there were any dwarves in her world, and whether men over the centuries had driven them so far underground that they were now completely forgotten.

As for our young heroes, I can happily report that they fared that whole day without incident and found a nice little spot to camp under a huge rock off in the woods a stone's throw from the road. It sheltered them from the rain. Lithglib managed to start a small crackling fire with wet tinder and left Ada to stir the coals under their supper—beef stew with carrots and potatoes—in order to help Racket set up the tents, which he couldn't have done a worse job with if he tried. Ada didn't mind. She was even beginning to enjoy herself. After a delicious meal, the sun went down and the crickets and fireflies came out, and the three settled into their tents, Lithglib and Racket into one and Ada into another just for her. She slept invisible, wrapped up in her voluminous cloak like a burrito.

CHAPTER EIGHT

WHEREIN THEY ARE DRIVEN FURTHER EAST

As you know if you've read anything by Professor Tolkien, dwarves love to make songs and poems. And so it should not surprise you that Ada woke in her tent to the sound of Lithglib singing, though not very loudly nor very cheerfully.

Alone from the fishing pond I went,
Although to me some friends were sent
To cheer me on from dusk to dawn,
Relieve my lonely banishment.

For I have ever been a fool
To fish in that unlawful pool,
Where the magic cup was standing up
Time out of mind by ancient rule.

A fool! A fool! I broke the spell
That made the waters of our well.
The chalice wrecked could not protect
The dwarves when their disaster fell.

Now monsters stalk the land, so bold
Now that the magic spell of old
Is broken! broken! Evil's woken
And dwarves now flee into the cold,

Into the dark, far underground,
Where e'er their strength is to be found,
But I, cast out, wander about
Friendless, faithless, and whither bound?

"You're not friendless, Lithglib," said Ada, coming out of her tent. "You remembered that at the beginning of your song. Don't forget it at the end."

Lithglib smiled, though Ada could tell his heart was not in it. "I didn't mean to wake you," said he.

"I'm glad you did," she replied, and sat down next to him as he poked the cinders of last night's fire with a stick.

After a while he said, "Are you ready for breakfast? There's still some embers in here. The rain stopped last night. I can find some dry fuel—or dry enough—and get the fire started again soon."

"Should we wake Racket up?"

"He'll wake up when he smells food."

"I wish I could help," said Ada. "Get us a rabbit or something." She pulled the sling out of her pocket and held it.

"Do you want to learn how to use that?" said Lithglib. "I've had one of those since I was a little child. Hyke taught me."

"Sure," said Ada. And so, before Racket awoke, and long before breakfast, Ada got in some practice with her sling. Lithglib was a good teacher. She used stones she found lying on the ground, not wanting to waste the perfectly smooth stones Hyke had given her. Lithglib set up some targets—pieces of tree bark and dead wood mostly—on top of a log. At first Ada was afraid of hitting herself, so she whirled the sling too far away from her body. At last, however, she stopped being afraid of it and slung a few rocks with the intention of hitting the targets, but more often they went either up into the air or straight into the ground. It was very difficult, and they decided to call it a day when Ada slung one rock behind her and knocked the kettle off a stump by the fire, causing such a clamor that Racket woke up and tore out of the tent in a terrible fright with eyes bulging (as if a goblin army were descending upon the camp). A good bit of laughter followed, even from Racket, who thought they had played a joke on him, and even from Lithglib, who was least disposed.

But Racket was not the only thing disturbed by the noise. Evil had followed them from Easelheath, and now a shadow fell across the land as dark clouds rolled over them from the west, though there had been clear skies only minutes before, and though Lithglib had started to make breakfast. There was a peal of thunder.

Ada was sitting by the fire on a stump next to the dwarves, when she heard a sound like something big moving in the forest behind her. She turned around and stared in that direction. At first she saw nothing, then—

"Lithglib, I see eyes looking at us in the forest," she said as quietly as she could, "just like before, when we were walking from the chief elder's house, before the bugs attacked."

"I see them," said Lithglib without looking (as far as

Ada could tell) and pretending to stir the pot.

"Me too," said Racket with a quiver in his voice. "What should we do, Lithglib?"

"I think they're boars," he said. "But they might be too big to be boars."

"I saw one as big as a cow in Easelheath, before the mosquitoes got him," said Ada.

Lithglib, in the same calm tone, said, "On my signal, climb to the top of the rock as fast as you can, Ada first. I'll go last and make sure you get up."

"Be careful, Lithglib," said Ada with feeling. She was beginning to tremble.

Whether he had been planning on giving the signal at that moment, or whether he had been startled by a sudden flash of lighting and thunderclap so close that it made the earth shudder, Lithglib suddenly yelled, "NOW!" and immediately the children sprang up and sprinted around the side of the rock, where they could climb up. At the same moment, a terrifying squeal issued from the woods, joined by others, and the boars were on them in a moment. Ada could hear them charge as she climbed the rock overlooking their camp. She was out of reach and Racket was off the ground and climbing when the first boar rounded the rock and came directly at Lithglib.

"Lithglib!" Ada cried.

At that moment, standing a few feet away, Lithglib took a run at the rock, ran three steps up the side, and grabbed onto a hold, just as the beast passed in a fury beneath him. The boars had six tusks and dead white eyes. Their hair was black and long like tarantula legs, and each was equal to a full-grown bull in size. They squealed in rage and returned to the children's camp and began rooting through their stuff. By this time all three children were standing on top of the rock looking down at the wild beasts squealing and trampling their tents and knocking over the pots and pans and rampaging everywhere. The boars were bolting down their breakfast, ripping open their luggage, and generally befouling, defiling, and destroying everything.

"Go away, you stupid pigs!" said Racket, throwing rocks at them.

"Don't waste those," said Lithglib. "Ada, can I borrow your sling?"

She gave it to him and the three smooth stones she kept in her pocket. With the ones on top of the rock, Lithglib had less than a dozen. He wound up and let one fly at one of the boars running about. It hit him in the side, but his hide was so tough that he only made a protesting grunt and continued to make a mess of things. Lithglib shot a few more times with as little effect. Then he aimed for the ones standing still and gorging themselves on their supplies. He whipped one rock with all his might and hit one of the beasts right in the eye. He squealed awfully and ran away half-blind, but stupidly came back a moment later and began again. Lithglib hit one on the nose, another in the eye, and the last right on top of the head, and then he was out of ammunition. The one hit on the nose just got angrier, the one hit in the eye ran off into the woods and never returned, and the one hit on the head—a perfect hit!— actually fell, but whether dead or simply unconscious they couldn't tell. The rest of the beasts continued about their business.

To make matters worse, it began to rain. Not the slow, drippy kind of rain like before, but the hard, fast, Noah's-ark kind of rain that comes down in sheets and drenches you to the bone. Huge explosions of lightning rocked the ground and lit up the sky. They saw the great arcs of light smiting the earth far too close for comfort. In all this the boars did not abate their destruction in the least.

And so three miserable children—two dwarf-boys and a human girl, to be precise—sat on top of the rock, huddled together and wrapped up as tightly in their cloaks as they could manage, though still soaked, and soaked again every time the wind whipped away a corner of their protection, and waited for their troubles to be over. At long last—hours it seemed—the storm passed on and the beasts got bored and trampled off into the forest. It was now sprinkling and the lightning was a long way off. All that was left was debris and the dead-or-unconscious boar, lying (as Racket did not fail to note) on top of his side of the tent. Finally, the beast woke up and scampered off after his friends, oinking smugly all the way.

"Well," said Lithglib, "we'd better salvage what we can. I'm sorry about breakfast, but it looks like it is going to be a long time before our next meal, unless we can find, hunt, or beg for it. We'd better keep going east."

CHAPTER NINE

WHEREIN THEY MEET A CONSIDERABLE FELLOW

"The Calix!" cried Ada, having a sudden fear. The three children slid down and jumped off the side of the rock and then ran towards their ruined campsite. The boars had eaten more than food. Tattered and rain-soaked remains of Ada's tent and pillow littered the ground, the kettle had been crushed by boar teeth, and the entire contents of their packs lay strewn about the place as if they had exploded.

"I found it!" said Racket, holding up the disenchanted chalice, oozing with boar slaver.

"Gross," said Ada. The one sapphire was still missing. It was unchanged, still as broken as ever. Although, now that she looked at it, perhaps it had changed after all. All the luster had gone out of it, and it was now just a dull old cup. Even the gems had lost their shine. And indeed, as they would find when it was clean and the sun was shining on it, it still looked rather shabby. Somehow this was just as discouraging as the loss of their things.

When they had salvaged what they could of their supplies, which wasn't much, and packed it away, which was difficult, since they had almost nothing to put it in, Racket said cheerfully and (as always) with perfect sincerity, "Look on the bright side: now we don't have to carry so much!"

The others smiled. "That's why we love you, Racket,"
said Lithglib. "You always see the good in things, even
when there isn't any to be found."

Racket beamed.

Ada was starting to get hungry now, and though they
had enough water (they now had only two water skins
between them), they would be getting weak and irritable
before long.

"Well," said Lithglib. "Let's hit the road."

This they did, careful to be on the lookout for hidden
enemies. The dwarves walked with their hands on their
swords and Ada with her hand on her locket, ready to
slide the lever down at a moment's notice. But nothing
came out of the woods, or nothing unusual, I should say.
Once a deer stepped out into their path, saw them, froze,
and then bolted off when they got closer. The rain and
the clouds had gone completely, leaving the grass, the
trees, and the children to dry as the warm sun came out
again. There are very few wholesome pleasures in life
more wholesomely pleasurable than basking in sunlight,
especially when you have been cold and wet, and Ada
was not insensible of this fact.

She was enjoying this, in spite of her hunger, and
her homesickness (which had just begun), when all of a
sudden the road stopped. They had seen from a distance
that it went up a small hill and had assumed that the road
continued on the other side, but when they reached it
they found that the road stopped right there and refused
to go a step further, even though the children must.

"Dwarves only make as much as they need when
it comes to mundane things like roads," was all of
Lithglib's explanation, which contained perhaps a little
irony. What they saw before them, however, was bright

and cheerful and beautiful. The country opened up into a vast golden meadow, skirted by little forests here and there, and the lofty peaks of mountains all around them. A fresh, invigorating breeze met them and lifted their spirits.

"We have to press on," said Lithglib, "even where there's no road, since there's no going back. Maybe we can find some berries in some of these forests." With that, they followed Lithglib down the short hill into the tall, golden grass of the meadow. Their green cloaks would not be much help if they needed to hide, not that that would be a problem for Ada. The grass was soft and came up to their belts, and it slowed them down a little bit. Ada walked directly behind Lithglib and followed in his steps. Her stomach growled.

The next day, after bivouacking under the stars with no more covers than their cloaks and no softer pillow than the earth, marching in the same direction, a smell came to them on the breeze, a strong and (to the uninitiated) very unpleasant smell, the smell of cattle.

Perhaps there was a farm nearby. Ada hoped so, for her hunger was starting to overcome her caution. Then they saw them. There were buffalo, dozens and dozens of buffalo grazing on the plain. They saw no fence and assumed they were wild, but they had nothing to kill one with, and nothing to cook it in if they did. It would take quite a shot to bring down a bison with only a sling. If only they had a bow. They had an idea of Ada sneaking up on one and cutting its throat, but she was too scared (and she didn't want to).

Then they saw something which made them duck in the tall grass and pray they hadn't been seen. It was a giant, striding slowly along some distance away, with a huge club resting on his shoulder. Luckily they were near a copse of trees, and they hide themselves inside before the giant looked their way.

Ada was already invisible by this time. With a brief rushing sound like a gust of wind, Ada vanished, although the dwarves could just barely make out her outline when she moved.

"Ada," said Lithglib. "Do you think you could get a better look for us? We'll be there in an instant if you're discovered." Normally Lithglib would never have asked her to do this, but even he was now growing desperate for food.

After much hesitation and some serious reflection on the possible consequences, she agreed. Why, after all, had she been given an invisibility locket if not for situations just like this? If she was unwilling to go on ahead and spy things out, she might as well hand the thing over to Lithglib, which she was most unwilling to do. It was her only real protection.

Ada crept very carefully and very quietly towards the giant, keeping to the shadows of the trees, in which she was truly invisible. Unlike most humans, who walk very loudly, Ada was quiet by nature. She was often told at home that she would make an excellent cat burglar, because no one heard her enter a room, and she often startled people when they turned around or looked up and saw her. That was when she wasn't trying. Now she was.

She saw that she could get fairly close—she felt no compulsion to get an inch closer than necessary—by sticking to the shadows on the edge of the woods. The giant was only a little ways away from the tree line, looking out towards the herd of buffalo—presumably his herd of buffalo.

When Ada got as close as she dared, standing stock

still in the shade of a large tree, she had time to observe his features, but unfortunately his back was to her. He was wearing a dirty, brown tunic that came down to his knees and was tied with a rope belt. It was frayed and holey in the back, revealing more than she cared to see. His skin was ghastly, ghostly white, but his hair, which was long, was black as black.

Then something happened which caused her some alarm. He turned around and started smelling the air in her direction, furrowing his bushy black eyebrows. Her fear of detection was increased by her disgust for his face. As the expression goes, he looked like he fell out of the ugly tree and hit every branch on the way down. His nose, if you can call it a nose, looked like a pig snout, or else like the absence of a nose. His eyes, which were like tiny black beads, were uneven and looked like they had retreated from his nose as much as possible to the sides of his head. He had a cleft lip which was so bad that, like his nose, it would tempt you to say that he had no upper lip at all. His pale gums and intermittent teeth were exposed. To perfect the image in your mind, add only warts and a very large and lumpy growth on his neck that pressed up against his jaw on one side. When he sniffed the air, his nostrils closed and opened repeatedly, which had the unfortunate effect of animating his face—the only thing which could have rendered it more hideous.

Ada recoiled from his ugliness and longed to slink back to her friends, but she did not dare to move, even in the shadows, as long as he was looking in her direction. Thankfully his attention was soon diverted back to the field and the buffalo, and Ada took the opportunity to sneak away. Her report did not set the dwarves at ease. Still Lithglib resolved to try to talk to him.

"Just because he's ugly doesn't mean he's bad," said Lithglib. "Maybe he's a good giant."

Racket was quivering from head to foot, and Ada was quivering from foot to head. Nevertheless, they agreed to follow him, though they were sure that they were far more likely to be eaten than to eat. They decided to stay near enough to the trees that they could run into them if they needed to but far enough into the meadow that the giant could see them coming from a distance. After all, the last thing they wanted to do was startle a giant.

They stepped out from the trees, and started to approach him. There was a moment of sheer panic for Ada when he spotted them. All of a sudden he crouched a little and put his free hand up to his brow to block the sunlight and gazed at them without moving, letting the head of his club rest on the ground. Ada didn't know if he was about to start running at them or not. Lithglib waved his hand over his head in as friendly and casual a gesture as he could muster. The giant just stood there stock still until they were within hailing distance of one another, then he dropped his hand from his head, stood erect, and raised the club to rest it on his shoulder. They didn't dare to flinch at this movement.

"Hello!" cried Lithglib, trying to sound cheerful, although his voice cracked. He cleared his throat and said again, more successfully this time, "Hello! My name is Lithglib. I'm a dwarf. What are you?" (He hadn't really thought about what he would say before he started speaking, and this was the best he could come up with on the spot.)

"A man," replied the giant.

"What sort of man?" said Lithglib.

"Such as you find," was the answer. The giant had a bass voice, not at all unpleasant to hear, which surprised Ada, since he was so unpleasant to see. Far from menacing, he seemed a little shy and awkward, as if he had not spoken to anyone in a long time and was trying to remember how it was done. He was taciturn at first, hesitant to speak. It was like he was looking for the right words, and testing them out in his mouth. He looked pained for a moment, and then Ada realized that he was conscious of the obligation to speak again. Perhaps he should ask a question.

"What are you?" asked the giant. This question had already been put to him, so he might as well put it to them, since he had not yet formulated an original query. (So he seemed to be thinking.)

"I am a dwarf," repeated Lithglib without the smallest hint of impatience.

"Yes. You said that," said the giant, merely indicating the fact. Then after another long, awkward pause, he added, "And what are they?"

"This is another dwarf, and this is a human."

"I have seen your kind, but not the other," said the giant, merely indicating the fact.

"What do you do?" asked Lithglib.

"These," said the giant, indicating the buffalo. "I keep them."

Lithglib spent the next minute or so nodding and looking off toward the buffalo, as he had run out of things to say. The giant exhaled deeply, and started to look not so stiff. As near as Ada could judge, he was starting to think that he was doing well for his first conversation in so long, though he was not certain. His next questioned confirmed her intuitions.

"I have not spoken in a long time," said he, "and I am unfamiliar with the custom. Pray tell me how I am doing. Is there anything I have left unsaid or should have said differently?"

"No! No!" said Lithglib. "You are doing very well! Very well indeed!"

There were sighs of relief on both sides, and now everyone was starting to relax. This was a gentle giant after all, just as Lithglib had said. Ada now felt bad for prejudging him. His manner was kind and even started to take away some of his ugliness.

"Guests!" said the giant so suddenly that the little ones jumped. "You are guests! I am your host, by right of ancient custom and by law of the gods. I am a god-fearing giant, you know, not a god-hating one, though most of us are god-hating. It is an ancient grudge, going back beyond the Great Flood, but I have turned from the wicked ways of my fathers and back to the ways of the First Men. And the gods tell us that all guests are to be treated as guests, and so shall I treat you, little friends. Pray tell me how many buffalo you can eat?"

"Just one will be more than enough for us!" said Lithglib. "Thank you so much for your kindness!"

"One for you and one for me, then," said the giant. "I have no house. God has given me only the fields and the stars in the heavens and the animals beneath them. For these things I thank Him. Do you thank Him?"

"Not nearly as much as I should, I am sure," said Lithglib sincerely, and a little guiltily.

The giant didn't seem to understand this answer, which sounded too much like impiety. But not trusting in his own judgment, he shook his head and returned to his former thought:

"I have plenty of buffalo, and buffalo you shall have."

CHAPTER TEN

WHEREIN THEY GET INTO A BIND

The giant put two fingers in his mouth and whistled two ear-splitting blasts, which Ada was sure could have been heard for miles and miles, if not from her own world. Presently two buffalo came forward from the herd, visibly trembling. When they were at his feet, he hefted his huge club and brought it down on the head of the first. He crushed its head in one blow and nearly knocked the children off their feet. The other buffalo retreated a short distance, but the giant ordered him to return by pointing his finger at the ground where he wanted it to stand. Fearfully the creature came back and dutifully received its death blow. Ada was astonished at the power he had over them, but she was so sick to her stomach that she had to divert all her thoughts to keeping herself from throwing up.

After this, the giant built an enormous bonfire, like a beacon in the night, whose flames seemed to reach the heavens. They had to sit a considerable distance from it so as not to be oppressed by the heat. On this inferno the giant cooked two whole bison. The children ate until their stomachs were bursting. They had been so hungry that they didn't even mind eating unsalted meat. Afterwards they lay on the ground under the stars, and the crackle of the fire after it burned down and the sound of the giant's breathing put them all to sleep. Ada did not sleep invisible that night. It was her fourth night away from home. With the god-fearing giant nearby, she felt more safe and slept more soundly than she had since she came into that world.

The next morning the giant loaded them with as much cooked buffalo meat as they could carry, wrapped in leather strips which he had tanned himself. During goodbyes, the giant said to them, "Go with the protection of the gods, little ones," then added in a more serious tone to Lithglib, "and do not leave off thanking them." They were thanking them right then for the giant's kindness. They did not bother asking him where to find the Sage, since they knew he had no knowledge of the outside world. They continued east through the golden fields.

"Darn," said Racket after the first mile, "We forgot to find out his name." That was true, but they were in no danger of forgetting him.

The dwarves were starting to get homesick, and it was made all the worse because they could never return. Lithglib started to feel his exile. He took out the Calix as they walked and looked at it. If possible, it had grown even more dull and lackluster. Ada wondered if it would rust or turn black. She wanted him to stop looking at it. Eventually he did, but his mood for the rest of that day was heavy and quiet. They found some wild berries and a clear spring to refill their water-skins. Ada got more practice with her sling. She could now fling rocks in the direction she was facing, but still couldn't hit anything. Lithglib had made his own sling out of a strip of leather given him by the giant. Though it was not as nice as

Ada's, his skill with it was much greater than hers. He killed a couple of squirrels, which he skinned and added to their buffalo meat, which was certain to go bad before they finished it. He kept the pelts.

"Do you think everyone is okay back home, Lithglib?" asked Racket as they were walking.

"I expect that they're holding out well under the chief elder's house, but they're probably starting to get hungry by now."

"Why hungry?" said Ada.

"Dwarves need to eat. Just because we can defend ourselves best underground doesn't mean we can grow food underground. I suspect most of their danger is in coming out for food, which won't last long with no one tending the fields and the livestock, if insects haven't eaten them all up already. The dwarves will probably migrate when they get hungry enough, so there won't be any Easelheath to come back to even if we could—or I could."

"We wouldn't go back without you, Lithglib," said Ada. "Right, Racket?"

"Right," said he, though less convincingly. Some time afterward, to break up the monotony of the march, Racket started singing a silly song:

I'm going on a journey with my two best friends
Far from home where monsters roam and laughter ends,
But never fear, our mission's clear: to make amends.
We'll find the Sage (if it takes an age) who all things mends.

There were many other verses like this before Lithglib finally had enough and told him to stop his drasty rhyming. Racket merely hummed after that.

Several more days passed without incident. Their

packs were getting lighter as they consumed the buffalo meat, which after a few days had gone bad and had to be discarded—another reason they regretted the loss of their salt, for salt preserves meat. But they found blackberries and wild apple trees, and Lithglib killed rabbits, birds, and squirrels. Ada took every opportunity to practice with her sling, and by the end of the week she had succeeded in killing her first squirrel.

"I hit it!" she cried, surprised to see one of her stones find its target.

Lithglib went over to examine it. "You killed it too," said he.

"Good job, Ada!" said Racket.

That night they held a celebration for her, although they didn't have anything extra (except ceremony) to add to their usual dinner. Lithglib, lit by the firelight and a full moon, raised his water-skin to her and proposed a toast, a toast which he never finished:

"Here's to you, Ada," he said, "friend of the dwarves, upon the occasion of your first successful hunt." Ada thought she heard some rustling in the bushes and instinctively put her hand to her locket. Lithglib apparently didn't hear anything, because he continued: "I for one am most glad you came to us when you did and decided to alleviate my lonely exile with your company."

"Hear! Hear!" cried Racket in agreement.

There it was again, the rustling sound. "Lithglib," she said, starting to get nervous.

But he went on: "We wish you health and long life. May our journey's end find you safe at home and—" He was cut off by a bag going over his head. Quick as quick, Ada had seen a goblin come up from behind him and put a bag over him. Ada had seen it coming, but she was too frightened to scream. Instead, she went invisible. (We don't get to decide how we react when we get surprised.) It was just in time, too, for a bag went over Racket an instant later, and a third, intended for Ada, came down on nothing but air, for she had scampered off to a safe distance. The third goblin looked into his bag, much confused, and then looked around, but Ada was totally invisible in moonlight.

The dwarves struggled admirably inside the bags, but the goblins tied ropes around the middle and lower part to arrest their arms and legs.

"What happened to the third one, Bolag?" hissed the first goblin.

"I could have sworn I'd nabbed her," said Bolag apologetically, "but look." He showed him the empty bag.

"You let her run off, you idiot!"

"Who are you calling an idiot, kin-slayer? She didn't run off. Somebody would have seen her. She just disappeared!"

"Tell it to the chief when we get back. We'll see what he thinks!" said the goblin that had bagged Racket. "Perhaps we'll have some goblin to add to our dwarf feast."

Bolag replied with fear in his voice: "No! I'm telling you, she just vanished! She must have been a elf, and I've heard they taste nasty anyway—all goodness and light and all that nonsense."

"Don't make excuses," said the first goblin, hefting Lithglib over his shoulder like a sack of potatoes. "Let's get back."

I cannot describe to you how afraid Ada was for her friends at this moment. All this put her in a state of mind which I hope she never has to experience again.

The second goblin put Racket, who was mumbling unintelligibly, over his shoulder. The third took their packs, and all three set off into the woods.

Not knowing what else to do, Ada followed at a distance.

CHAPTER ELEVEN

WHEREIN ADA IS CLEVER

Things happened too quickly before for me to describe the goblins to you, but now that Ada is following her friends and their captors, we have some time. The goblins were black as sin with hairless and shiny skin. They had big, oval-shaped, bloodshot eyes, little, sharp teeth, no lips, and long pointed ears, and they were taller than dwarves, though not as tall as men, especially because they always walked bowlegged and crouching, sometimes with the assistance of their hands, except that now they could only use one since they were carrying the dwarves and their luggage on their backs. They wore black and rusty armor but no shoes and wielded clubs and curved swords called scimitars. They sounded like snakes when they talked and hyenas when they laughed. I dare not describe their stench to you, but know that it was profound. They were the wickedest creatures that Ada had ever seen, heard, or smelled.

She could see well in the moonlight, which was lucky, because she could not use the locket both to be invisible and to see in the dark (since the silver slides over the lens to make a full moon). She followed them for hours. Their songs were as vile as their persons and not worth repeating.

Finally they ran out of forest. By this time Ada was weary after a long day's march followed by a long

night's march at a brisk pace with no sleep. They came
out onto an old cobblestone road overgrown with weeds
and ivy and missing stones in many places. It led them
toward a dark structure, a castle, which stood alone on
the plain with the moon above it. It was windy and
cold, and Ada pulled her cloak closer. The sound of
the wind in the trees behind her was eerie and caused
her to look over her shoulder to make sure nothing was
coming up behind her on the road. As they approached
the black castle, Ada observed that it was just as much
in a state of disrepair as the road. The gate was fallen
down, and there were holes in the wall big enough to
walk through. The parapet at the top of the wall was
missing stones like a mouth missing teeth. She followed
the goblins through the open gate into the courtyard, or
rather the boneyard, since it was littered with bones as
far as the eye could see. The castle tower had collapsed,
taking out an enormous section of the wall and leaving
a mountain of rubble in the gap.

The original occupants of these ruins were now long
gone, and the goblins had taken up residence there—for
goblins don't build; they take. Soon the goblins turned
off to the side and went into an open doorway down into
the dark. Ada hesitated as she came to the threshold.
The wooden door had rotted away ages ago. Ada's eyes
could not pierce the darkness, and she was afraid to
switch to her locket's other function. She listened for
a moment but heard nothing. The clinking of goblin
armor and the patter of soft goblin feet on hard stone
had quickly faded away underground. It was now or
never.

Ada looked around to see if there was anyone outside,
then slid her locket open, put the lens to her eye, and
started to descend the stairs, more afraid than ever, but

bravely resolved not to let her friends get eaten by goblins if there was anything she could do about it. Her heart pounded. She was alert. As before, when she looked through the lens, the passage appeared to be bathed in moonlight. It quickly grew colder and damper as she descended, and the stone walls echoed. She moved as quietly as she could, but her foot loosened a stone from the crumbling stairs, which proceeded to skip down the steps to the bottom, echoing frightfully. Ada was sure that she had been heard, but when she listened, she still heard nothing. She felt guilty for not moving faster, afraid of what might be happening to Lithglib and Racket as she stood there starting at echoes. She continued down until she came to the bottom. There the passage turned a corner to the right. She stopped and listened, then, hearing nothing, she peeked out with her locket. She saw a long, unoccupied passageway and the bars of many cells on the left and openings on the top-right from which the moonlight poured in. It was enough to see by, so she went invisible and walked quickly and quietly down the hall, looking into each cell as she passed. There were bones in many of the cells, skeletons still shackled to the wall. Ada almost ran past them. When she reached the end, still not finding her friends, she had to go down another dark stair and switched her locket accordingly.

In this fashion she searched the dungeon until she heard the echoing sounds of the goblins again. Now she stayed invisible even in those parts where she was blind. Luckily, when she got closer, she found that the goblins had lit torches and stuck them in sockets sticking out from the wall. She followed the sounds of their voices until she turned a corner and found them. They were in a little room straight ahead rummaging through the children's belongings, from which room they could see the cell on Ada's left into which they had thrown the dwarves. There was a space in front of their cell too, a square area cut into the wall, which had a bench in it and some torches and instruments of torture hanging on the walls. Ada snuck up to the bars. Lithglib and Racket were sitting against the wall, their ankles shackled and chained to an iron hook in the middle of the floor, their faces downcast. They had been stripped of all but their underclothing. They could not look more wretched.

Ada whispered as quietly as she could, "I'm here." In fact, she whispered too quietly; they hadn't heard her. So she whispered again as loud as she dared, "I'm here. It's Ada."

That time they heard her. Both instantly looked up. Racket could have shouted her name, but he restrained himself. Perhaps Lithglib had warned him.

"Ada," whispered Lithglib. "You'd better get out of here. It's too dangerous. If you see Hyke or the Backets again, tell them I'm sorry." Racket, who was not so quick to resign himself to death, stared openmouthed with undisguised horror, looking from Lithglib to where he supposed Ada to be.

"I'm not going to give up on you, Lith—" started Ada.

"Knock off that whispering in there!" said one of the goblins in the other room so suddenly that Ada thought she had been discovered. But they went back to what they were doing, and Ada and the dwarves tried to be quieter.

"Where is the key?" asked Ada.

"The big one that grabbed me has it," whispered Lithglib.

Ada now turned her attention to the goblins. They

were rummaging through the things and arguing amongst themselves.

"Why can't we eat them now, or just one of them?" said Bolag. "He can't know how many we caught."

"By Mephistebub and Beelzepheles! You are just spoilin' to get yourself killed!" said the big one. "First you let one go; now you want to try and cheat the boss!"

"I'm just saying. He doesn't know how many we took."

"Do you think you'll make more sense if you keep saying it?"

"Well, can I at least keep one of these swords or cloaks, or even this old cup. I'm sure he wouldn't want it."

"If you don't shut up, I will kill you where you stand," said the big goblin, snatching the Calix from his hand and—to Ada's frustration—handing it to the other goblin, saying, "Take this to the boss and tell him what we've caught, all of it!"

"Of course all of it," he replied. "Don't think I'm as big a fool as this one here." Ada got out of the way as he slunk through the doorway and around the corner, disappearing with the Calix.

"Lithglib!" whispered Ada, a little too loudly.

"I know," he said. "I heard."

"I thought I told you to shut up!" said the big goblin, storming out of the room. Ada fled into a corner. He took a short whip with several knotted lashes off a hook on the wall and opened the door of their cell with one of the keys on an iron ring which he took out of his pocket. He was in such a hurry that he left the key in the lock.

It was frightful to watch, but he whipped Lithglib and Racket several times. They couldn't get away because they were shackled to the floor, and they cried pitiably with each blow. Meanwhile, Bolag stood outside the cell, holding onto the bars and laughing and jumping up and down with glee and wagging his tongue at the poor dwarves. Luckily Ada kept her head; otherwise she might have done something foolish. Instead she did something clever.

When the big goblin had given each of them several sharp lashings, he came out of the cell and slammed the door closed behind him.

"Where's the key?" he said, looking down at Bolag.

"What do you mean?" said the smaller goblin.

"I mean what I say! Where is the key? I left it in the lock. What have you done with it!"

"Nothing! Nothing! I swear on all that is unholy. I didn't touch it!"

"You're planning on eating one of them, aren't you? You said it yourself."

"No! Never! I would never! Maggog—you talked sense into me. It would be stupid to try to cheat the boss. I know that now!"

"Hand it over," said Maggog, "I'm giving you one last chance."

"I don't have it! I swear! I—"

Maggog had had enough. He now brought the whip down on Bolag, who cried and whimpered and tried to get away. He crawled into a corner—Ada's corner! She darted out of it just in time. Bolag danced about, covering his head with his hands, as Maggog whipped him.

"Give it back, worm!"

At last Bolag escaped around the corner, down the hall, and up the stairs, cursing all the way.

"One of these days," said Maggog, "he'll make a

much better roast than he ever made a goblin." He tried the dwarves' cell door, but it was locked (Ada had locked it during Bolag's scourging). He was puzzled and angered. "Drat! Now I'll have to break the lock," he said, and went away, probably to get some tools. For the moment, however, he was gone.

— CHAPTER TWELVE —

Wherein They Get Out of a Bind

When the goblin was gone, Ada ran to the cell, unlocked the door, and went to her friends. Lithglib and Racket were groaning, lying on their sides because their backs hurt. Ada reached out her hand and thoughtlessly touched Racket, drawing it back suddenly when he cried out in pain.

"I'm sorry!" she said. "Are you okay?"

"We'll make it," said Lithglib, sitting up. "Come on, Racket, we need to get up."

"We need to hurry!" said Ada. "He could come back any moment."

Lithglib and Racket got up, but the latter wouldn't look at her, for he was crying—not so much from the pain as from being whipped.

"I'm sorry, Racket," she said. "You're very brave. We have to go now."

Racket simply nodded, and the dwarves ran into the side room to collect their gear while Ada kept watch.

"Quick!" whispered Ada. "I think I hear him coming!"

"Just swords, Racket," said Lithglib. "I have a plan." He quickly related his plan to the others, and then everyone took their positions.

Maggog the Goblin was having a very good night. He had captured two dwarves and a lot of loot for the boss, and he had whipped a traitor. He had taken off his helmet, and was whistling as he returned to break the lock on the dwarves' cell, imagining himself parading them and their belongings in front of the goblin chief. He was expecting a promotion. He was expecting some of the treasure. He was expecting a fair helping of dwarf. He was *not* expecting the dwarves to be gone!

Maggog stopped whistling when he turned the corner and found the cell empty. But oddly enough, even though he had stopped whistling, he could still hear whistling, though of a different sort. It was coming from right behind him. He turned around, but did not at first see what it was. Then he saw it, and being a very superstitious goblin, he froze. There was a disturbance in the air, like a wheel made out of wind or water, spinning around and around, moved by a little ghostly hand in the middle. The spinning and whistling sped up and then suddenly stopped, and the next thing he knew, a stone hit him right in the throat, knocking the wind right out of him. After that the dwarves were on top of him with their swords—and ended what had started out to be a very good night.

By now you have guessed Lithglib's plan, which had gone off with perfect success. Ada didn't even have to hit the goblin; she only had to get him to turn around, giving the dwarves time to attack him from behind. It was a bonus that they found him on the floor clutching his throat and gasping for air. The dwarves finished him off without trouble. Ada, visible again, was now at her leisure to be sick. She had seen far too much nastiness of late. They were all a bit traumatized and ready to be out of danger.

"But we can't leave just yet," said Lithglib as he cleaned his blade of the black goblin blood. Ada had forgotten about the Calix.

"Can't we just leave it, Lithglib?" pled Racket. "It doesn't work anyway."

"You two should get out of here while you have the chance. I can't leave without it."

Ada grew a little angry now. "Stop saying that, Lithglib. We're not leaving you. And besides, you don't know the way out, and you might need our help." To tell the truth, Ada didn't exactly know the way out either, but she had a much better idea than he did.

The dwarves put on their cloaks and their packs, which, though not nearly as heavy as they were at the beginning of their journey, hurt like the dickens after a whipping.

"If we live," said Lithglib, "I shall have to finish your toast, Ada. It will have grown rather long by the time we're through, and I imagine it will have become a song."

"This way," said she, and the three children went around the corner, down the passage, and up the first stairway. It was not difficult to find the way out; they just had to keep going up. And it was not difficult to find the goblins; they just had to follow the smell. And the noise. They decided to be certain about their escape route before they went after the chalice, and when they reached the air and the sky again, it was morning.

"Good," said Lithglib. "The goblins won't want to follow us into the light. We just have to make it to the surface."

"After we steal the chalice," Ada reminded him,

for that task was almost certain to fall to her. She immediately regretted saying this, because afterwards Lithglib made another apology and gave her another chance to leave him.

"We're with you all the way, Lithglib," said Racket, who meant it but still didn't understand why they needed to go back down to the goblins.

After they stowed their packs outside the castle gate, they went back in and down again into the dungeon and soon found the main room where the goblins were. Since it was well after dawn, all the goblins were sleeping on the floor. It looked like a massacre, the way they lay in total disorder. The smell was almost too much to bear. They were snoring loudly, lying with their arms and legs and even whole bodies on top of each other, crossed, crisscrossed, and intertwined. Every once in a while one would give a sharp kick and another would shout, growl, or hiss, and then go back to sleep. Ada would have to pick her way carefully through all the goblin arms and legs.

"Look," whispered Lithglib, pointing toward a bigger, uglier goblin sleeping on a throne in the middle of the room on top of a raised platform. He was holding the Calix lightly in one hand, almost letting it drop. "I think I can make it," he said.

Ada was intending to volunteer, but the sight of all those goblins filled her with dread, and so she didn't.

"Be careful, Lithglib," said Ada, then very reluctantly but because it was the right thing to do, she offered him Diana's Locket.

"Are you sure?" said Lithglib.

"Yes. You need it more than I do right now."

"I'll bring it right back," said he, slipping it over his head and sliding it closed. Nothing happened.

"Here, let me try," said Ada, opening and closing it again. Still nothing happened. For a moment she was afraid that it was broken, but when he gave it back to her and she tried it on herself, it worked just fine.

"Maybe it only works for females," said Lithglib, "or humans. Hyke did say it might have come from your world. That's all right. I don't need it." And before Ada could say anything, Lithglib had taken his first step into the room, putting his foot down carefully between two sleeping goblins. Ada and Racket looked on anxiously. Very carefully he stepped over one, then another. In this fashion he made his way across the room towards the throne. Once he came to a point where he had to leap to get to a clear spot. He put a little too much force into his jump, landed off-balance, and almost fell on top of a pile of goblins. Ada had to remind herself to breathe again. Another time a goblin wrapped his arms around Lithglib's leg and tried to use his foot for a pillow. It must have smelled like food, because he started licking it. Lithglib slowly extricated his leg. The goblin grumbled but did not wake.

Finally Lithglib reached the throne. He moved as slowly as he could with knees bent and hands out towards the goblin chief. Ada could hardly bear to look. Lithglib reached out and slowly began to lift the cup from his hand when the worst thing happened: the chief goblin, feeling himself lose his grip on the cup, grabbed a tight hold of it and stood up, although it took him a second to come to full consciousness. When he did, there was a moment of shock on both sides as the goblin and Lithglib stood toe-to-toe, each holding onto the goblet and staring each other in the face. Lithglib was saved by sheer luck, for in the next instant, with both his hands gripping the cup, he did the only thing he could do: he stomped on the goblin's foot as hard as he could. The goblin chief howled in pain, released the Calix, grabbed his foot, and started hopping up and down on the other.

Lithglib was not expecting a reaction quite that strong. He did not know (since he had never read George MacDonald) that goblins' feet are their weak spot, or as we say, their Achilles' heel. But Lithglib did not miss this opportunity to escape. He dashed off the platform and started running overtop of the sleeping goblins. Between the chief goblin's cry and Lithglib's stepping on them, the whole room began to wake up. If they had woken up instantly, he would have been a goner for sure, but goblins drink too much and eat too much and as a result they don't wake up too much—I mean, they wake up slowly and disoriented and with a splitting headache. By the time any of them were aware enough to give chase, Lithglib was at the door, and the three of them sprinted down the hall and up the stairs to freedom.

They heard the fury of the goblins behind them, but once the children were out in the sunlight and the clean air, the goblins ceased their pursuit. The children heard angry protests coming from the dungeon entrance, but none of the goblins dared to come out into the day.

CHAPTER THIRTEEN

WHEREIN THEY MEET A DIFFERENT KIND OF STORYTELLER

Retrieving their packs from their hiding place, the children spent the rest of that day putting as much distance between themselves and the goblin dungeon as they could, heading east (according to their compass). They were afraid that when night fell, the goblins would come out and hunt them down and kill them. They wanted to keep going through the night, but since none of them had gotten any sleep the night before, and since they had been walking, running, and worrying for two days straight, at last they had to stop. At sunset, all three of them threw themselves down in a cave accessible only from a shallow stream and immediately fell asleep, not even bothering about supper or keeping a lookout.

When Ada awoke, it must have been past noon, for the sun was reflecting off the brook in a wavy pattern on the ceiling. She could not see herself and realized that one of the dwarves must have closed her locket while she slept. She opened it, reappeared, and sat up. And the first thing that she noticed was that she was alone. Utterly alone. Even their luggage was gone.

"Lithglib? Racket?" she called out, standing to her feet. There was no answer. Her first thought was that they had been recaptured by the goblins, and she quickly closed her locket again, even though it was broad daylight outside. She called out to them again, a little louder this time, but there was still no answer except her own voice echoing inside the cave. Now she was really beginning to worry.

"Please, God, let them be okay," she prayed in a whisper. She crept to the mouth of the cave and looked outside. The light hurt her eyes. She looked up and down the stream that ran by the cave but didn't see them, and the trees on the wide banks were impenetrable walls of green. The water tumbled and skipped down the rocks in the middle of the stream bed, which deepened as it went, though the water was still only ankle-deep.

Invisibly, Ada followed the little brook downstream in hopes of finding her friends. She had no training in this kind of thing, but she thought she detected dwarvish footprints now and then in the soft dirt. The banks rose up on either side and made her feel trapped. The roots of the trees above her hung down into the channel. She would have to use these to climb out if danger appeared.

But danger did not appear, and she walked for several minutes without seeing any sign of her friends. She was just about to turn around and head upstream when she came upon a shiny object on the ground. It was their compass, but it was broken and no longer pointed east (as all dwarven compasses do). It had survived the boars, but it had not survived the fall. It must have slipped out of Lithglib's pack and fallen on the rocks. Why hadn't he heard it and picked it up? And why had they abandoned her? She teared up a little, but I hope you will not think any less of her for that. No one likes to be left behind, whatever the reason.

She picked up the compass, and it disappeared into

her pocket. She looked around and saw, through the trees, the roof of a little cabin in a low clearing. She climbed the bank and went down a hill towards it as stealthily as she could. It was a dreary old shack with dark, weather-stained wood and a soggy, rotting roof. The awning had collapsed on one side, and there were wooden planks on the ground leading to the porch. The planks served as bridges over the mud at the bottom of the hollow—thick, black mud with flies and gnats skittering along the surface. Ada was afraid that if she fell in, the mud would swallow her alive. It did not smell lovely either.

Ada reached the edge of the swamp and now had to go across the planks. The fact that she was invisible made it difficult to walk, since she couldn't see her feet. She only saw where her shoes made an impression on the dried mud. She held out her arms as she went across. Once she almost fell in, as she misjudged where her foot would land. It slipped off the side of the board and upset her balance. She recovered herself before she went in the mud, but the board lifted up on the other side and came down again, knocking against the rocks on each end. It sounded louder to her than it really was, and she froze and looked at the front door to see if it would open. When it didn't, she proceeded across with more caution.

Finally she made it to the porch. The floorboards creaked treacherously as she stepped on them, no matter how slowly she moved. By this time she could hear talking from inside the shack. Ada snuck up to the cracked and dirty window and looked through a hole in it shaped like a claw. This is what she saw.

Lithglib and Racket were quietly sitting on the floor, still as death, listening to the story of an old dwarf with a long nose and a longer beard, which reached down to his knees. The old dwarf had an evil look about him, and hopped from one foot to the other as he told his tale (a little too sprightly for a dwarf of his age). There was a crazy look in his eye, and his voice rose almost to a squeak whenever he got excited by what he must have supposed were the best parts of his story.

His story, which I won't repeat, was an awful tale about some nasty, wicked children who make plans to kill their father so that they can have the house to themselves and do as they please. The heroes and the villains were all mixed up. The dwarf praised the wisdom and the cleverness of the children as they plotted their murder. The worst part about it was that he was such a good storyteller (or else some kind of magic was at work) that even Ada started to feel that the children were, after all, rather clever. But what was she thinking? They were going to go kill their own father! But on the other hand, maybe he had it coming; such attractive and charming children as these must have good reasons for what they do. And they did sound so nice.

As you can see, the spell was already beginning to work on Ada. If she had waited around any longer, she would have fallen under it completely and been stuck there just like Lithglib and Racket. Thankfully, she realized what was happening to her and moved away from the window and beyond the power of his voice. She shook her head violently to get the mean and selfish thoughts out of it, but they continued to bother her for some time afterwards, and she felt guilty whenever they came to her.

You see, this dwarf was one of those nasty, wicked kinds of storytellers whose books (in our world) get mixed up with the good ones and accidentally picked up by children, or by their parents, teachers, and librarians. I'm afraid to say that these kinds of books are becoming all too common nowadays, and it is getting harder and harder to tell them apart from the good ones, most likely because many grownups have forgotten that it is their duty to try.

Anyway, Ada managed to break free from the dwarf's spell and now stood at a distance trying to figure out how to break her friends out of it. Since no better plan occurred to her, and since she wanted to free the dwarf-boys as soon as possible, she decided to break the window. First she went back across the planks so that she could get away if she needed to. Then she felt around in her pocket. There was her sling and the broken compass. That would work. By touch alone, since she was still invisible, she loaded the sling with the compass. By now she had grown so familiar with it that her fingers knew what to do all by themselves.

Standing about forty feet from the shack, Ada began swinging the sling around and around, which made the whistling sound she knew so well. Finally she launched the compass, which crashed through the center windowpane of the cabin. The sound startled her and she flinched, but otherwise remained stock still. She heard a heavy tread on the floorboards and suddenly the front door burst open. The evil dwarf looked out and about, fuming with anger. In one hand he held the compass, in the other no better a weapon than a rolled up manuscript. Ada's heart leapt into her throat whenever his eyes crossed the spot where she was standing, but he never saw her.

When he was satisfied that the vandal was gone, the dwarf beckoned to Lithglib and Racket, whom Ada could see through the open door. Only then did they move.

The two dwarf-boys stood up, shouldered their packs, and followed the old dwarf out the door and across the planks. Ada moved to the side to let them pass and then proceeded to follow them.

"Now remember what I told you," said the old dwarf, handing the rolled up manuscript to Lithglib as they walked. "Give that to the Professor and to no one else!" And then after a moment he added, "And don't tell him who it's from until he's had a chance to read it."

"Yes, Mr. Lillipupan," said Lithglib and Racket in unison. Their voices were as expressionless as their faces. They were still under his spell. Ada would have to try something else.

CHAPTER FOURTEEN

WHEREIN THEY MEET THE PROFESSOR

Ada was still hatching plans to break the spell on her friends when they arrived at wherever it was that Mr. Lillipupan was taking them. They had walked for the better part of an hour through the woods on what looked like a deer path. At the end of it, the trees stopped suddenly, and through them Ada saw the grandest old house she had ever seen, which I shall describe in a moment.

When he reached the forest edge, Mr. Lillipupan turned on his heel and repeated the instructions which he had given before. Then he snapped his fingers loudly, and the boys seemed more awake and less like they were in a trance, although still not at all like themselves.

At this point, a stately she-dwarf with cat-eye glasses standing by the house spotted Mr. Lillipupan and started walking in his direction. She walked with a cane and with authority. Mr. Lillipupan growled, hissed, and fled, and finally Ada was alone with her friends again, if only for a moment. When she was sure that the evil dwarf was gone for good, she opened her locket and appeared next to them.

"Lithglib! Racket! It's me, Ada!"

"You again?" said Lithglib gruffly and without surprise. "I thought we'd gotten rid of you."

"That's right, Lithglib," said Racket, "I couldn't have said it better myself. What she is still doing here fumbling up all our plans, I have no idea. Why, I was just thinking the other day—"

"Shut up, you," barked Lithglib.

Ada teared up instantly. Although she knew they were not themselves, it hurt worse than you can know to hear her best friends talk like this to her. (Sadly, some people in our own world, who are under no particular spell but their own, talk like this to their friends all the time.) Ada was spared the pain of continuing this conversation by the arrival of the she-dwarf.

"Who are you children and what are you doing here?" she demanded.

The dwarf-boys instantly changed their moods, and Lithglib said with pretended sweetness, "We're here to see the Professor, ma'am. We've heard so many good things about him. May we see him, ma'am, and may we compliment you also on your very fine garden? I have never seen its like."

The she-dwarf was taken aback by this, and she looked into their faces and started to examine them shrewdly.

"Please, ma'am," said Ada, "they are not themselves. Mr. Lillipupan has done something to them."

"I see that," said the other. "That old scoundrel. I wonder that my husband hasn't done something about him yet. Well, don't worry, little one; the damage isn't permanent, although I daresay they're going to feel pretty rotten when they're cured."

"Then there is a cure?" asked Ada.

"Oh yes. There's nothing better for driving out a bad spell than a good one. You're in luck: my husband's literary group has just arrived. If you three will come along, I'm sure you'll be in for a good story. Oh! but we have not been introduced. I am Mrs. Clark. Welcome to Brickworks!"

"My name is Ada. This is Lithglib and Racket. They're from Easelheath."

"Pleased to make your acquaintance. Come inside and meet my husband."

"We are here to speak to the Professor, ma'am," said Lithglib with little warmth.

"My husband is the Professor, you silly fool," said Mrs. Clark. "Now come along and meet him."

Now that they had started towards the house, I am at leisure to describe it to you. And now that Ada was assured that her friends would be cured, she was in the proper spirit to appreciate it.

Brickworks was a long, two-storey, red-brick house with a red-tile roof and bright, white windows, brighter and whiter than you can imagine. Above the windows on the ground floor, the gables were covered with leafy vines which had grown all the way up to the eaves. The windows in the upper storey projected straight out from the long, sloping roof, from which three red-brick chimneys stood up proudly. But before you could even get to the house, you were met with a fecundity of verdure (that is, a lot of green and growing things). There was a garden that defied description—nevertheless, it contained yellow, red, purple, violet, and blue flowers, and was itself contained by hedgerows of perfectly groomed, perfectly rectangular, green bushes. The colors were bright, and the greenness of the garden and the redness of the house were the brightest. The light was dazzling. It was like heaven. It was like coming home. It was like nothing Ada could compare it to. Her heart leapt inside her with joy as she took it all in.

As they came around the side, they saw a gigantic, red-brick oven connected to the house. Mrs. Clark, acting as their tour guide, said it was called a kiln and was used for firing bricks or making whatever else the Professor asked for.

"Brickworks takes its name from this kiln," said she.

But more wonders were still to come. On the other side of the house were more hedgerows, and a stream, and down the hill a ways, a hot air balloon!

"You have a hot air balloon!" cried Ada in astonishment.

"Of course," said Mrs. Clark.

Ada didn't know how she hadn't seen it before, sticking up from behind the roof. It was the same color as the bricks. As the four of them were standing there, the burners flared up all by themselves, sending a long jet of flame into the balloon to keep it full of air, while the basket remained anchored to the ground by means of rope. Ada was delighted and amazed, but Racket and Lithglib were insensible to everything. She felt sorry for them and hoped they would be able to properly appreciate things before they left.

On their way into the house, they met the gardener. He was digging near the rosebushes with a spade, and he was aided in his efforts by a little guinea pig with a red ribbon tied around the middle like a bow, digging along beside him.

"Good morning, Mr. Ford," said Mrs. Clark.

"Good morning, ma'am," said he, looking up from his work. He was a plump dwarf whose face seemed to be permanently marked by concern, even now, when he was obviously trying to express delight.

"Fine weather, don't you think?"

"Fine at the moment, Mrs. Clark," he said, looking up at the sky, "but I expect the rain will come soon and wash away all the top soil and kill the vegetables. If we don't drown, we'll probably starve. But it hasn't happened yet and there isn't anything we can do to prevent it, so we might as well keep our chins up and be merry while we can." He said "merry" in so un-merry a tone that Ada wondered if he really meant it, or if all his merriness was on the inside and too shy to come out, for she got the feeling that he wasn't half so gloomy as he seemed.

"Good day, Mr. Ford," said Mrs. Clark.

"Good day, Mrs. Clark," he replied, tipping his cap to her. With that, they took their leave of him (not without a strong desire on Ada's part to hold the guinea pig), and the three children followed Mrs. Clark into the house.

Upon entering, they were greeted by a clean-shaven dwarf with big, egg-shaped glasses and the kindest face Ada had ever seen. He stood up from behind the desk at which he had been writing and organizing papers.

"This is our secretary, Mr. Wolper," said Mrs. Clark.

Mr. Wolper came around from behind his desk and, with both hands, began to shake theirs with feeling. "So very pleased to meet you," he said with the utmost sincerity.

"This is Ada, Lithglib, and Racket," Mrs. Clark continued. "The latter two have been to see Mr. Lillipupan and are here to speak to the Professor."

Mr. Wolper obviously understood her meaning, for his manner changed to one of concern and pity, and he shook the boys' hands as if expressing his deepest condolences.

"Thank you, Mrs. Clark," said he. "I will show them upstairs." And so he did. As they climbed the stairs, Ada got an excellent view of the interior of the house, which was every bit as grand as the exterior. There were paintings, coats of armor, busts and statues, axes and shields, ancient manuscripts framed in glass, and ancient tools, arrowheads, coins, gems, and bits and bobs of every description inside glass display cases. It was rather like a museum. The handrail and spindles were made of dark, finished wood with a delicious smell and feel, which terminated in a curl around a little ornate lion sitting at the top of the banister.

When they reached the top of the stairs, Mr. Wolper slowly opened one of two double-doors and peeked into the room. Through the crack, Ada saw a bunch of very eminent-looking dwarves sitting around a circle with a fire crackling in the fireplace.

"I'm sorry to disturb you, Professor, but we have guests," said Mr. Wolper.

"Well, bring them in!" said one deep voice like a belly laugh.

Mr. Wolper opened the door to admit the children. The three of them went in and were invited to sit on a thick, comfortable rug near the fire, since all the armchairs were taken. The big dwarf with the big, merry face was obviously the Professor, although from the looks of the others, he was not the only one with that title. Mr. Wolper handed him a hastily written note. After he read it, the Professor turned to the children and said,

"I understand that you have come to speak with me, children, but if you'll excuse me, we have just started our meeting. Professor Tobit was just about to read a composition of his which he has lately finished. We'll talk after he tells his tale. May I offer you tea and biscuits? They're right behind you on the table."

After that, he urged Professor Tobit to begin his story, which he did. Ada, who sat warm and cozy with a blanket around her and her back to the fire, had to listen closely, because although Professor Tobit read out loud, his voice was not loud at all, and he read much too quickly. This is the tale he told.

CHAPTER FIFTEEN

WHEREIN THEY HEAR THE TALE OF CEDRIC THE GENEROUS

Cedric Mac Allan was a wealthy man, sister-son of the King of Banfilns, in the land of Alms Matha, near the castle Mannonacht. Cedric lived in a stately house on yon hill in the Matha, and with him lived his pretty wife and two plump sons.

"Go trade that old mule," said his wife one day, "and get something good for it. And let it be unshod when it's sold."

"That seems like a good idea to me," said Cedric. And out he went with the old and shoeless mule, pulling it by a tether to the market. Well, while he was still on the road, Cedric saw a sight. On the side of the road, there was a horse stuck in the mud and three men trying to pull it out. "No time to help them," said Cedric to himself. "And if I get myself all muddy, the wife won't let me sit down to dinner."

Not long after, he saw another sight—a goose with bagpipes stuck in its throat and a woman trying to pull them out. The goose was tooting and blowing and making a terrible noise, half goose and half pipes. The woman looked at Cedric passing on the road.

"No time," thought Cedric, "and the goose has gone and done itself in, anyway."

Then he saw a third sight, and this one was a wonder. A pig wearing a hat was up a tree. Several men below were jumping up to try to grab hold of it, but the pig went on squealing and holding on to the branch with three legs and its hat with the fourth.

"No time, no time for anything but a laugh," Cedric said to himself. And by he went, laughing and dragging his old mule by the tether.

When he reached the market, he found a rich man wearing a suit with green and white stripes. But what caught Cedric's eye was the glass jar he held in his hands, which contained solid gold in the shape of a woman's face.

Cedric called to the man: "To your family's honor, sir!"

"And to yours!" returned the rich man.

"I want to buy that jar of yours with the gold face in it. I have this sturdy mule for trade. He's—uh—younger than he looks."

"Oh, but this is a special jar, you see," said the rich man. "It was made by fairies. If you take the gold face out of it and put the jar before a mirror, in the morning there will be another one inside, as surely as your heart is true and your hands are useful, my good friend."

"Take this mule and anything you ask!" cried Cedric.

"I'll take that old, shoeless mule and your wife and your two sons for it," said the rich man.

"You ask a hard price, but they are yours." Cedric exchanged the tether for the jar, and at once took to his heels and ran home to flee the country with his wife and sons. But when he opened the door, he found his wife changed into a goose and his sons into a horse and a pig.

"This is a hard price indeed," said Cedric.

"This is what happens to a cheat," said the gold face in the jar.

"Is there anything to be done?" pled Cedric.

"Speak to the king of Otherworld," said the gold face.

"Where is he?"

"In Otherworld, of course!"

"How can I get there?" asked Cedric.

"You can't," said the face.

So Cedric went and put his wife and sons in the barn, and put rings in their ears to tell them apart from the other animals. The goose was hardest to manage. She honked furiously and nipped at Cedric's hands.

Then he went inside his house, removed the gold face from the jar, stashed it with his other gold, and put the empty jar before a mirror. Then he drank until he was half drunk and fell asleep. The next morning he went to see the jar, and there was another gold face inside, just like he had been told. But when he took it out, he found that it was only butter. Then he went to his hoard of gold, but all of that had turned to butter too.

"Curses on the rich man!" he cried, and shattered the jar on the floor. All in a fury, Cedric went to find his shoes, but they were nowhere to be found; so he went out without them. Uttering curses, he took the road to the market. But while he was still on the road, a dark mist came over him, and when the mist parted he was in Otherworld. There was a great castle upon a hill in the distance, with a road leading up to it. And on either side the grasses of the meadows were colored in stripes of green and white. Well, up he went towards the castle, and he passed many strange things on the way.

First he saw an old, blind man sitting in a doorframe.

There was no house and no door, just an old, wooden doorframe and a few stone steps crumbling into the road. Then there came a man walking by on legs that were ten feet long and straight as stilts. Hearing him, the blind man crawled out to beg.

"I have nothing for ye!" said the long-legged man, but just then his purse fell from his belt and the gold spilled all over the ground. His legs were so long that he couldn't reach down to get it, and the blind man tried to gather up the gold. But every time he groped along the ground, the long-legged man stomped on his fingers and caused him to give a sharp cry.

"Why are you stepping on the blind man's fingers?" said Cedric in anger.

"I can't reach my coins, but he will never have one!" said the long-legged man.

And as grievous as this was to Cedric, he left them to it and went on. Soon he saw another sight. There was a woman in the road with bare feet, and she had a hundred toes on each foot all the way around. One foot was stuck in a rut under a wagon wheel. She tried and tried to push the wagon off her, but it would only roll back on her foot and cause her to cry pitiably. Well, not fifteen feet away was a bench facing the road, and on it sat three lazy boys with great big arms and small hands. One sat on his hands, another leaned back with his hands behind his head, and the third was asleep with his hands folded on his chest. The first two just kept watching the trapped woman without expressions on their faces.

As grievous as this was for Cedric, he held his tongue and continued up the road until he saw a third sight. As he was crossing a bridge, he saw a little child flailing about in the shallow stream, drowning in two feet of water. On either side of the stream, there was a huge statue of a stork with gems for eyes.

"Why doesn't somebody save the child!" cried Cedric. And just at the moment when the words left his mouth, the two stiff-necked birds bent down and dipped their beaks in the stream, whereupon the water went down and disappeared entirely. The little child ran away laughing, and Cedric continued on his way.

When at last he reached the castle, he saw a fourth wonder. There were two French knights standing outside, calling over the castle wall and confessing their love to two fair maidens leaning out from the windows of their towers. The maidens were faint with love, but the knights were not allowed to enter through the gate, nor could they get over the wall. So they paced back and forth, rent their hair, pulled their beards, and gnashed their teeth.

Then from the forest on the right came a giant, and the trees parted and the ground shook as he walked. "Don't eat me!" cried the first knight, and his maiden screamed. But the giant gently knelt down and picked up the knight. He stood up and reached over the wall to put the knight in the maiden's tower, but even the giant's arm was too short. So he pulled his arm out and held it up with the other one, and the knight got in. As soon as he had done so, the giant's arm disappeared, and he sat down against the wall and rubbed his shoulder.

Then from the pond on the left a fairy emerged, glowing like evening clouds and sparkling like a whole constellation of stars as she flew towards the second knight.

"Don't change me into anything unnatural!" cried the second knight, trembling, as she alighted next to him. But she plucked off her wings and put them on the knight, and he used them to fly up into the window of the second tower, where his maiden waited for him. And as soon as he was up, the wings disappeared. The fairy's light went out, and she went and sat in the giant's hand.

"Wonder of all wonders!" Cedric exclaimed, and he passed through the gates and entered the castle. There in the great hall were many princes, nobles, beggars, and lepers, all drinking and talking and laughing together. There was a long carpet with green and white stripes, which led up to the steps of two thrones, whereupon sat the King and Queen of Otherworld. The King bid Cedric come forward, and he did, kneeling on the step.

"What is it you have to say?" said the king, and the court fell silent.

"Explain to me the meaning of the four wonders I have seen, and how I might change my wife and sons back to human form."

"The meaning of the four wonders you have seen is this," said the King. "The long-legged man represents those who do not give when asked. The three lazy boys are those who do not give unasked. The stone storks are those who give when asked. And the giant and the fairy are those who give unasked."

The king's words were like a sword that split Cedric's heart in two. "I am unworthy," he said. "Do not return my wife and sons to me. Only give me generous hands."

"I will tell you how to change back your wife and sons. A twelvemonth from the day you sold your old and shoeless mule and tried to cheat the rich man at the market, take your wife and two sons and walk them around your land three times without shoes on your feet. Then go and beg three silver coins, and place one in each of their mouths, tying up each beast in a different cave.

After that, walk backwards up the hill to the well of Alms Matha, kill the man you find there, and throw him into the well. When you have done so, you will find your wife and sons in their true forms."

After the King of the Realm spoke these words, the dark mist encircled Cedric and then disappeared, and he found himself back in his own house. A twelvemonth passed, and he followed all of the king's instructions. But when he walked backwards up the hill and turned around, he saw a man made out of pure gold on the other side of the well. When Cedric approached the well, the golden man approached too, and stood the same distance from it. Then Cedric saw that the man was a mirror image of himself.

When Cedric walked around the well to meet him, the golden Cedric walked the other way, so that the well was still between them. The gold Cedric copied his every move. No matter whether he walked forward or backward, around one way or the other, he could not reach his golden self. Ten years passed, but still Cedric could not catch himself; so finally the two stood on the edge of the well and jumped at each other. They fell for a long way with their hands around each other's necks. The moment the gold Cedric hit the water, he melted away like butter. The well water steamed and erupted like a geyser, shooting the real Cedric up over the houses of Alms Matha and down through the roof of his own home.

When he awoke, he found himself in his own bed with his wife and sons standing over him in their true forms. From that day forward Cedric was the most generous man in Alms Matha, and his neighbors wanted for nothing which was in his power to give, whether from the gold in his pocket or the strength in his hands.

CHAPTER SIXTEEN

WHEREIN A GOOD SPELL DRIVES OUT A BAD

By the time Professor Tobit finished telling his tale, Lithglib and Racket were in tears, not because it was sad, but because the magic of it had driven out Mr. Lillipupan's spell and left them feeling pretty rotten.

"We're so sorry, Ada!" cried Lithglib and Racket together.

"Can you ever forgive us? We abandoned you," said Lithglib.

"It was Mr. Lillipupan!" cried Racket. "We couldn't help it!"

"I forgive you guys," said Ada. "I know it wasn't your fault. I almost got spelled too." This wasn't quite the right word for it, but Ada had grown up in a world where magic had become rather rare, and so she lacked the proper vocabulary.

The scene was quite touching, and the circle of dwarves let them hug and cry it out without saying a word. When it was over, the Professor—that is, Professor Clark, who owned Brickworks, and who was the only dwarf referred to by his credentials alone—turned to Professor Tobit and said,

"Well done, Tollers. I knew you were the right man for the job. Mr. Lillipupan's enchantments are quite nasty indeed, if not very strong. What a bother of a man! I shall have to put up a notice or warning of some sort, if the King doesn't return to these parts soon and do something about him.

"Well," he continued, lighting a pipe, "I suppose introductions are in order, now that you are all yourselves again and in your right minds. I am Professor Clark, and this is Professor Tobit"—who gave a slight bow, though he kept his chair—"And this is my brother, the Major"—who was just calling the Secretary to bring up a bottle of mead from the cellar, and calling his present beverage "detestable varnish."

The Professor continued: "Over here we have Mr. Field, Mr. Hill, and Dr. Humpty"—the last of whom wore a bowtie and really was shaped like an egg (Ada had of course read Lewis Carroll). He was the first dwarf whom Ada had seen with hair neither on his chin nor on his head.

"My name is Lithglib, and this is Racket. We're from Easelheath. And this is Ada. She is a human from the World Inside the Trees."

"Fascinating!" cried several of them.

"You must have quite a story to tell," said the Professor. "Let us hear it, and we will do everything in our power to help you."

That they did. Lithglib spent a good part of the afternoon telling them their tale. In the meantime, Ada availed herself of the Professor's invitation to have tea and biscuits, though she was surprised to find that they were not biscuits at all but cookies. The Professor and the other elder dwarves listened with eagerness, excitement, shock, and concern at all the right parts of Lithglib's story. More than ever, Ada felt like she was home. And safe. She didn't even wish for her chapstick. The Major drank his mead, and the Professor drank cup after cup of tea, each with at least six lumps of sugar. Every once in a while he would tap some ash from his pipe onto the carpet and rub it in with his foot. Once, when Mrs. Clark came in and witnessed him do it, she scolded him, but the Professor only replied that ash was good for carpets.

"It keeps the moths away," he said.

The dwarves were very polite and asked Ada all about her home and her family and life in her world and how she got to theirs. They expressed their sincere pity when she told them about when she was lost in the cold and the dark before she received help from the dwarves. They expressed their sincerest astonishment at Lithglib's story of how he broke the Calix and let loose monsters all over Easelheath. The Professor examined the chalice with the keenest interest as Lithglib related his banishment and their setting out on their quest for the Sage on Mt. Heofon. All the elder dwarves expressed wonder at Lithglib's mention of Diana's Locket and required a demonstration, which Ada was happy to give. She disappeared, which caused them to gasp, and then reappeared, which caused delighted laughter and applause on all sides. Even Racket applauded, overcome by the gay and festive mood in the room. Ada curtseyed for them all.

When Lithglib told them about their swords, Professor Tobit exploded with rapture: "You have Naegling and Hrunting! You have them with you! Stars above! May I see them!" Whereupon Lithglib and Racket produced their swords.

The Professor, turning his attention from the Calix, laughed and said, "You have caused our dear Professor Tobit unspeakable delight. Naegling and Hrunting are very important to his work."

"My good boy," Professor Tobit said to Racket, turning on him sharply. "There is goblin blood on this blade. That is no way to treat a sword of this antiquity. You will remember to clean it properly in the future?" This was more of a command than a question.

"Y—yes—yes sir," said Racket nervously.

"The scabbard is going to need a good cleaning now too," said Professor Tobit, returning their blades to their sheaths and their owners.

Lithglib continued his story. When he got to the part about the giant, the Major exclaimed, "A god-fearing giant, you say! Wouldn't that be a jolly fine friend in a row with the goblins! If only we'd had that kind of artillery behind us when I was an infantryman in the goblin wars of 1792 to 1815...." He rambled on for a little while, reminiscing about his military days, and Lithglib politely waited for him to finish before he continued his story.

When Lithglib got to the part about their own experience with goblins and how he recovered the cup from their chief, the Professor exclaimed, "Ha! Tollers, I told you goblins had soft feet!" Professor Tobit grumbled something inaudible in reply.

Finally Lithglib got to the part of the story which Ada wanted to hear herself, the part where she got left behind and the dwarf-boys fell under Mr. Lillipupan's spell. By this time, Racket was in such a good mood that he could not be contained, and he helped his friend tell what happened.

"Racket and I woke up before Ada. We were refilling our water-skins in the brook, when we saw a stranger walking up from a little ways downstream—"

"Tell them what you did next, Lithglib! It was so clever!" interrupted Racket.

"I pretended like I hadn't seen him and went back into the cave to close Ada's locket, since she was still asleep, just in case he was dangerous. When I came back out, he was already talking to Racket—"

"He had such a nice voice!" said Racket. "You just wanted to keep listening—"

"Even when his story grew wicked," interrupted Lithglib.

"Yes," said Racket, "but you just had to know how it ended!"

"By now I had been taken in as well," continued Lithglib. "Mr. Lillipupan said that we would have to follow him back to his cabin to hear the rest of his story. We were so far under his spell that we forgot all about Ada, which was lucky—for her sake." At this point he looked at her with his familiar expression of affection, sympathy, and guilt, all rolled into one. She put her hand on his. Mr. Hill and Mr. Field were particularly moved by this gesture of friendship.

Lithglib went on: "As I climbed up the side of the stream bank, following Mr. Lillipupan, I heard what must have been our compass fall out of my pack, but I was in no mood to climb down and pick it up."

"Which is very unlike him," interrupted Racket. "He would definitely have picked it up if he hadn't been under a spell."

You and Ada know the rest of the story, and the rest of the room soon knew it too, including Mrs. Clark and Mr. Wolper, who had stayed to hear the end.

When it was over, the whole room applauded. Ada was starting to detect the delicious smells of supper being prepared downstairs.

"That is quite a story!" said the Professor. "You've had a fair bit of adventure so far, and I'll wager that you have a fair bit more before the end. If my nose does not deceive me, the cooks have prepared an excellent supper. Do stay at Brickworks tonight. I daresay Mrs. Clark has already ordered the maid to prepare rooms for you. You have? Ah, that's a good she-dwarf! Tomorrow we will talk about how best to speed you on your way."

The children thanked him from the heart.

"Oh, one last thing, sir," said Lithglib, taking Mr. Lillipupan's manuscript from his pocket. "This is his manuscript, although I don't know if you want it now, knowing who it's from."

The Professor took it from him and gave him back the Calix, then carelessly leafed through a few pages. Ada was not afraid that he would fall under Mr. Lillipupan's spell. Somehow the very idea seemed absurd, like the idea of a moth annoying an elephant or a mountain. Soon the Professor made a sound of disgust and annoyance, got up, and threw the manuscript into the fire.

"Mr. Lillipupan is not a bad writer in one sense, but the worst kind in another. If he thinks that this patricidal, regicidal, deicidal rubbish is going to earn him a chair in this room, he deceives no one more than himself."

CHAPTER SEVENTEEN

WHEREIN THEY ARE SPED ON THEIR WAY

Dinner was delightful. The whole household was in attendance, including the gardener, who remarked that the food was excellent but lamented that it would probably run out. He also noted the warmth of the fire but regretted that the smoke would probably give them all tuberculosis. Ada at last got to hold the guinea pig and held him throughout the whole meal and fed him lettuce from her plate. Dr. Humpty was so fat that he would not have been able to reach his food if they had not cut a semi-circular section out of the table for him long ago (like Thomas Aquinas). The elder dwarves, especially the Professor, told many jokes and anecdotes, some of which Ada didn't understand, but she laughed all the same, so overcome was she by the joy and merriment of the room. There was laughter all around the dining room. There were chuckles from every chair. There were giggles and snickers in every nook and cranny. The Major drank, mumbled, and drank. The Secretary laughed modestly and with the greatest deference. The Professor sat at the head of the table with his wife and Professor Tobit on either side. Mr. Hill and Mr. Field raised their glasses to their host and drank to his health, which prompted Dr. Humpty, Mr. Wolper, and the children to do the same.

Ada sat between Lithglib and Mr. Wolper. Racket was lost in the general mirth, but Lithglib kept glancing towards the door as if he were expecting someone. Ada thought he might still be afraid of Mr. Lillipupan, so she asked him about it.

"It's nothing," he replied.

After dinner, Professor Tobit, Dr. Humpty, Mr. Field, and Mr. Hill bid the Professor goodnight and farewell till next Thursday and were escorted to the door by Mr. Wolper. It was night outside, and Ada was getting tired. The Major had fallen asleep in his chair with his ponderous chin on his ponderous chest and his head lolling to one side, snoring mightily. The maid chose this as the safest moment to confiscate his drink. After she returned, Ada was happy to find that their rooms were ready for them. After Ada received a blessing from the Professor, the maid took her upstairs first and showed her into her room. She helped her into a nightgown and lit a candlestick and handed it to her. Ada felt just like a girl in a fairytale. The maid, after asking if Ada needed anything else and receiving a negative answer, told her that she would be just down the hall if she needed her in the night, and then closed the door behind her.

Brickworks had a good night atmosphere about it. Ada had never been in a place where she felt less likely to get the creeps. Good life was lived there. If it was haunted, it was haunted by good spirits. Just knowing that the Professor was in the house made her feel safe. Ada blew out her candle and fell asleep.

The next morning, after a warm bath, Ada joined the dwarves for breakfast. The maid had poured her a bath in a bathtub in her room and laid out her clothes, which had been cleaned—all before Ada woke up.

"This is like the Grand Hotel," thought Ada, though she had only been to Mackinac Island once and had only been allowed to see the hotel from the outside.

Breakfast was much quieter than dinner, though no less formal. They were still served the fanciest food by the kitchen staff, and they had far more silver plates, silver bowls, and silverware than they could use. (It was a fecundity of silver.) The sun and the breeze and the song of birds came in through the windows and the open door, through which Ada could see the garden.

The children ate breakfast with the Professor. He said that his brother, the Major, would probably not be up for several more hours and would not appear until early afternoon. Mrs. Clark had already had breakfast and tea and had begun her second patrol of the grounds.

Ada caught Lithglib glancing outside every once in a while as he had done the night before, but she did not ask him why.

"Now I suppose we should get down to business," said the Professor, after they had eaten. "I have already had my staff replenish your supplies, which are waiting for you by the door, for I perhaps more than anyone understand the importance and urgency of your quest. You see, I happen to know quite a lot about the Calix. What dangers you have left behind are not only greater than you have seen, but they will reach farther than you know. Not only Easelheath will be destroyed if all is not set to rights again. And soon! The evil will spread to all the surrounding countryside, and indeed, will reach further and further every day. Up till now you have been able to outrun it, but—come outside with me."

They did so, and this is what they saw. The garden, the lawn, the meadow—indeed, all of the Professor's grounds were green and bright as a spring day, just like the day before, but beyond the western boundary and creeping around to the north and the south, the trees were starting to change colors and lose their leaves.

"Fall comes early this year," said the Professor, "for it is not yet summer. Brickworks is protected by magic, but soon the evil will surround us."

"When will it stop!" cried Lithglib quite unexpectedly. He had not, Ada knew, allowed himself to forget his crime or its consequences for a single moment since their journey began, and this fresh manifestation of it brought him nearly to the point of despair.

The Professor looked on him with pity and waited until this pang of emotion was over before answering. "I'm afraid it will never stop till the Calix is restored," he said.

"Where is Mt. Heofon?" said Lithglib in a lower voice. "I must get to the Sage as soon as possible."

At this, there was an unaccountable smile from the Professor, which Lithglib didn't see, because he looked down at the ground, though he would certainly not find the Sage there.

"I'm afraid the Sage no longer lives on the mountain," said the Professor. "Or so I have heard. He is frequently in this country now, however, and might turn up any day. But you daren't wait for him. Even if you ran into him in the next five minutes, he wouldn't be able to help you fix the chalice. He needs materials to work with. There's a sapphire missing from your cup; that'll have to be replaced. If I were you, I would see if I could get my hands on a magic jewel which goes by the name of Pucelle's Heart. It was last seen in Bulverton, a town to the south of here. I wouldn't send you to that place if I could help it. You'll have to keep your wits about you."

"Why's that, sir?" said Racket. Lithglib was too depressed to speak.

"Bulverton is both ridiculous and dangerous— the worst combination, if you ask me. I'm writing a biography of its founder, though it's more of a warning about the town. Whatever you do, don't try to talk sense to them; they'll just lock you up as a madman or do something worse to you. Try to keep your heads down, and don't do any more talking than you need to." Racket seemed to think that this last warning was for him, and he said no more.

Unfortunately, this seemed to be the only information the Professor was going to divulge on the subject. Perhaps it was better if they didn't know the true nature of Bulverton. At any rate, he went on.

"You're also going to need to acquire a bottle of Frisian Myrrh. The king of the Frisians owes me a favor for taking care of a little monster problem for him some time ago. If you mention my name, I'm sure he will give you a bottle."

"You killed a monster, sir?" said Racket with undisguised astonishment, looking at the old dwarf. Ada was embarrassed on behalf of her thoughtless friend.

"Why, yes," said the Professor. "Lastly, you're going to need linen."

"Linens?" said Ada, confused.

"Linen," confirmed the Professor.

"We have that at home," said Ada. "We make sheets out of it."

"I'm afraid the material is far more rare here," said he. "Linen is made from flax, a rare plant with blue flowers. I'm afraid I don't know where to send you to look for it. At any rate, I have written you a list"—which he handed to her—"And here is a map"—which he also handed to her. "That should help you find Bulverton and Friesland. I will try to track down the Sage. Perhaps it's best if you all return to Brickworks once you obtain those items."

All this time Lithglib did not look up. The weight of his guilt was heavy on him. He did not even speak, though it was the polite thing to do, which was most unlike him. Ada and Racket thanked the Professor on his behalf and made their goodbyes. Ada hoped beyond hope that she would indeed get a chance to see him and Brickworks again. The Professor blessed them, with a special blessing for Lithglib, and took his leave.

Lithglib mechanically followed the other two to get their things, and then they headed south away from the house. Before they left the grounds, however, Lithglib stopped and looked around for a moment. Ada could not help herself:

"What are you looking for?" she asked.

Lithglib sighed. "Hyke," he said. "He said he would catch up with us. I hoped it would be here."

"I'm sure he's all right, Lithglib," said Ada. Racket concurred.

"Maybe," said Lithglib.

"Is that why you were looking outside last night and this morning?" said she.

"Partly. Also—" He paused, as if it were a labor to speak. "I could feel the darkness coming."

CHAPTER EIGHTEEN

WHEREIN THEY COME TO BULVERTON

As the children reentered the forest, this time headed south, Ada could feel the same evil, the same watchful eyes on them that she thought they had left behind in Easelheath. As I said, the trees had changed colors overnight and began to lose their leaves, but not in the same way as in the Fall. This was a different kind of Fall entirely. Although the leaves first turned red and yellow, they quickly lost their pleasant colors and became shriveled and gray. They disintegrated and blew apart in the wind like burnt paper. There was a snow of ash which got in Ada's hair. The birds had gone again, leaving an uncomfortable silence in their wake, and the insects started to grow in size. Already the mosquitoes were the size of beetles. No doubt the animals of the forest would soon undergo their transformations into monsters.

Ada pulled her hood up. Its rings were so small that not even the mosquitoes could penetrate them, but she wasn't completely covered, and she still got a lot of bites. They itched terribly. Ada knew that it was no use to go invisible, since mosquitoes hunt by smell. She wished she had dwarf skin now. Whether because their skin was so tough, or whether humans are sweeter, the dwarf-boys seemed not to get eaten up as much. What Ada wouldn't have given for some magic bug repellent!

As they walked along a little-worn path, she noticed that the creeping vines began to cover it more and more. She hated walking on them; she was afraid that they would wrap themselves around her feet like snakes. But they didn't. Not yet, anyway.

The worst part about the mosquitoes was that they distracted her from keeping a lookout. She was afraid that their annoyance distracted her from her true danger, and she looked around as often as she could to see if anything was watching them from the trees. With one hand she held her locket and her cloak; with the other she touched her little dagger. Her hood impaired her peripheral vision and made her look over her shoulder even more frequently.

Lithglib, although he walked in front, seemed to sense her state of mind. "Don't worry, Ada," he said. "We're safe for the time being. And don't you worry, either," he said to Racket, who looked around just as often.

That night they camped off the side of the road with a big fire to keep the bugs away. They slept in the new tents which the Professor had given them. Ada made them promise to wake her if they intended to leave camp or fall under the spell of an evil storyteller. Lithglib humorlessly agreed and made another unnecessary apology. Ada had a hard time sleeping that night because she was so itchy; and of course, scratching only made it worse.

The next day, when they awoke, the forest looked, if possible, even grayer and deader than before. Without a word, all three packed up camp as quickly and quietly as they could and started south on the road. They wanted to reach Bulverton before things grew any worse, but what they would do once they left there they had no idea. If things got as bad everywhere as they were in Easelheath, it was doubtful whether they would be able to finish their quest. The thought seemed to weigh heavily on everyone as they trudged along at a brisk pace. Ada, though weaker than the dwarves, was aided in this by her longer legs.

Just about lunchtime the road straightened out and they saw a city in the distance. There was a wall with a gate in it, over which they could see the roofs of houses. It was a colorless city, like something out of a black and white film. And as they approached, Ada noticed that the color seemed to fade out of everything. The green of the grass seemed to vanish. The red of a bed of roses planted alongside the road seemed to lose its brightness. This was a different kind of magic than that which pursued them, for even the green of their cloaks and the color of their eyes turned to corresponding shades of gray.

"What is this, Lithglib?" inquired Racket with trepidation as he looked at his colorless self and his colorless friends.

"I don't know," was the answer. But they didn't dare stop, for now they were within sight of the gate guards, who were waiting in a guard shack for them to approach, and they wanted to appear as natural as possible. Ada pulled back her hood. She prayed that they would have no trouble there, but as they got closer, she had not much hope of that.

"Lithglib!" she whispered. "One of the guards is a goblin!"

"I know," said he. "Try to act natural." Acting natural for Ada would have involved going invisible and running away, but she understood what he meant and obeyed.

"Halt there!" cried the other guard, a dwarf, as both came out to meet them. Both guards looked ridiculous. The first, a swag-bellied dwarf, wore long riding boots that came up almost to his hips and a drab cut-across coat that fit him a little too snugly and caused his gut to spill out over his breeches. He had no beard but instead a moustache that stuck out to the sides and curled upwards. On his head he wore a dark cap with a rose-shaped ribbon for a badge (called a cockade), and in his arm he held an oddly shaped spear, like a musket with a bayonet on the end. The goblin looked even stranger in such clothes, which, far from taking away his savageness, only added a kind of pompous absurdity to his appearance and made him look even more frightening because of it. He crouched and stank as all goblins do, and his kneecaps stuck out from holes in his soiled, white gaiters. On his head, instead of a cap, he wore a black hat in the shape of a football cut along the stitching (called a bicorn), which hat was always slipping off its owner's head and needing to be readjusted. All this was made more frightening still by the black and white, horror-movie atmosphere, for by now there was no color left in heaven and earth.

"Halt there!" cried the dwarf, lowering his spear at them as he approached. "Who are you and what do you want?"

"We are travelers," said Lithglib, "and we want to pass through Bulverton. We don't intend to stay any longer than we have to." He didn't mean this as an insult, although it certainly sounded like it. Ada hoped the dwarf-guard wouldn't get offended, but now she had other things to worry about, for the goblin-guard skulked around them as the other spoke, sniffing them and (as Ada thought, with a shudder) wondering how they might taste. She could feel goblin breath on the back of her neck, and it was all that she could do not to scream. She gripped her locket tight.

"That is as may be," said the dwarf-guard dismissively. "Where's your gate tax?"

"Gate tax?" said Lithglib.

"Do I stutter? Yes, gate tax! The tax for going through the gate!"

"I'm sorry," said Lithglib, "I had no idea. I'm afraid we don't have any money"—which was true.

"You have other goodss besidess money," hissed the goblin, stretching a claw towards Ada's shoulder. This was too much to bear. Ada recoiled with a shriek and retreated into Lithglib. Instantly the dwarf-boys moved to protect Ada, standing back to back with her between them and their swords half drawn.

"Stop! Stop! Stop!" cried the dwarf-guard. "Enough! Jacques Five, leave them alone!" The goblin whined to his much smaller companion, "You're so mean to me, Jacques Two!" and disappointedly slunk back to the guard shack. The dwarf-guard rested his spear on the ground and looked around nervously.

"Fine, no tax this time!" he said bitterly, "But I'd better not hear that you went to our superiors about this, or we'll come after you!"

With that, and with much doubt on the children's part about whether they should enter the city at all, Jacques Two opened the gate and admitted them.

CHAPTER NINETEEN

WHEREIN LITHGLIB ASKS A QUESTION

The children huddled together just inside the city gates. Before them was a long paved road which leaned to the left. With much trepidation and unease, and hesitating for a long time, they moved as one body down the street. This is what they saw.

On either side of the road were houses with white picket fences—this in itself was not alarming. What was alarming were the gates of these fences, which looked like white doorframes with the blade of a guillotine suspended at the top. Paranoid and suspicious eyes peeped out of windows. Paranoid and suspicious doors slammed shut. Across the walls of four houses in a row was written the following phrase (in what Ada hoped was paint): LIBERTY—EQUALITY—FRATERNITY—OR DEATH. Many dwarves and goblins were hurrying along the street. Many horse-drawn carriages went clippety-clop on the paved stones, but some of their goblin drivers whipped the poor beasts into a gallop and raced down the street.

One such goblin, driving like a lunatic, flew down the street as if pursued by the Hound of the Baskervilles! The pedestrians jumped out of the way to avoid death under the hoofs and wheels. The children almost didn't see him in time, and at the last moment they dove off the road. Racket dove the farthest and fell under the blade of the nearest guillotine-gate. Whether by magic or mechanism, the blade fell. Ada saw it, as it were, in slow motion, but there was nothing she could do about it. Racket saw it too, and with a dim-witted look of surprise and faster reflexes that she thought him capable of, he rolled out of the way just as the blade sank into the ground. The rope trembled. After a second, it began to ratchet the blade back up to its original position.

Ada and Lithglib pulled Racket to his feet. The latter touched his head to make sure it was still attached, which it was, though he had lost a few curls. He had the same look of astonishment on his face, although now all the color had gone out of it (that is to say, it was several shades whiter, since there was still no color in the world).

"That was a close shave!" laughed Racket, though he was so shaken that his teeth chattered. "That was two close shaves!"

Ada's heart was still thumping in her chest.

"We'd better stay to the side of the road," said Lithglib in his bravest tone. So they walked in a narrow line between the precarious carriages and the precarious gates. Ada walked closely behind Lithglib holding onto his cloak. She looked around her every few seconds with heightened senses (like a frightened animal), always afraid someone or something was going to jump out at them. The goblins were the worst. Many of them wagged their tongues at them as they passed. Ada's every muscle was so tense that her body ached, and she kept looking for a way to get off the street and hide.

They met a lot of people on the road, all of whom seemed to have the same name. Jacques Ten, Jacques Fifty-Three, Jacques One Hundred and Fifty-Seven.

There was a little more variation among the women, all of whom were also numbered, and were named The Vengeance, The Fury, Harpy, or Gorgon. They had a crazed look in their eye, and the children avoided talking to them as much as possible. Many of them wore dirty aprons and dirtier knives in their girdles, and all the citizens of both races and genders wore the dark caps with the rose-shaped badges.

"Death to the Royalists!" went up the occasional shout. Or worse, "Death to the King!" Ada jumped whenever someone nearby blurted out one of these unexpected and savage cries.

She also saw an occasional giant taking big, slow strides down the road, but she had no reason to hope that they were god-fearing giants, and if there had been any doubt, one episode in particular confirmed her suspicions forever.

One giant, who had been coming their way (causing them to dart off the road), stopped by the side of a wine shop, slowly bent down, and much to the owner's chagrin, picked up a full barrel of wine. As the shop owner and his customers stabbed in vain at the giant's feet with knives and pitchforks, the giant crushed the barrel over his head, sending a great quantity of wine-dark rain into his mouth and onto the heads of his diminutive assailants. At this point the pain in his feet must have reached his brain, because the giant bellowed loudly, lifted up his leg, and stomped the wine-shop owner flat—with a shock that knocked the other attackers on their rumps and caused all the guillotines in the neighborhood to fall at the same time. After that, the giant continued on his way, and the citizens, on hands and knees, lapped up the pools of wine in the road with their tongues.

The three children, huddled together and hiding in a

shop door, had waited for the fight to end and the giant to pass by before trembling on down the street. They gave the wolfish drinkers a wide berth. If it had not been so light out, Ada would have closed her locket, but she would have drawn more attention to herself if she walked around looking like a water spirit.

"Who can we ask about Pucelle's Heart?" whispered Ada in despair. No one seemed safe.

Lithglib, mistakenly taking this as a reproach, stopped the next she-dwarf he met.

"Please, ma'am," he said. "We—"

"'Ma'am'!" she said in a flash of anger. He was not off to a good start. Ada hid behind Racket. "Is that how you address me! How would you like to be denounced at the nearest Section?"

"I'm sorry!" said Lithglib, almost calling her ma'am again. "We're not from around here!"

"Humph!" she humphed. "We have no titles or privileges here! You address me as citizeness! My name is Harpy Eighty-Two!"

Lithglib refrained from pointing out that "citizeness" was just as much a title as "ma'am." "Citizeness," he said, "thank you for helping us foreigners get along in this fine city of yours. Perhaps you could tell us why there is no color?"

"Color?" Harpy Eighty-Two looked puzzled. "Ah, yes, I seem to remember something about that once. Quite a lot of folk used to believe in such nonsense, most of them Royalists. Are you a Royalist!" She cried with sudden suspicion.

Lithglib thought it best to deny the charge.

"Ah, well, you'd better get yourself a cap of Liberty

then. Anyway, many people used to think that they saw some strange quality in things which they called 'color.' Then Citizen Bulver came (may his name live forever) and taught us that 'color' was only in our minds." She got dreamy-eyed and even a little teary-eyed at this reflection.

"I see," said Lithglib. Then, finally getting around to the question he wanted to ask: "Citizeness, have you heard of a jewel called Pucelle's Heart?"

At this Citizeness Harpy Eighty-Two stared blankly for a moment, then suddenly laughed out loud, though it was neither very genuine nor very pleasant. "There is no such stone," she said. "It's all in your head. You probably once had a friend named Pucelle whom you were in love with. That's where the heart comes in. No doubt she wanted nothing to do with you, and you were in such a state of mind about it that you gave yourself brain fever, had some very confusing dreams, and woke up with a belief in this imaginary jewel!"

Lithglib didn't dare to contradict her. Ada had no idea what all this had to do with the stone. There was no need to invent this ridiculous explanation; the dwarf could have just that said she'd never heard of it.

CHAPTER TWENTY

WHEREIN THE CHILDREN ARE DECLARED ENEMIES OF THE STATE AND CONDEMNED TO DEATH

Ada wished now that Lithglib had been more careful in his selection of a citizen to talk to, although they might have walked from one end of Bulverton to the other and never found anyone more sane and civil. There was an inward savageness about the she-dwarf who called herself Harpy Eighty-Two which always seemed to be in danger of coming out, and coming out in a burst of violence that would be impossible to predict or prevent. She wore a knife in her belt, and it bothered Ada profoundly not to know the color of its stains. For these reasons, Ada hid behind Racket during the interview, since she did not feel safe with only Lithglib between her and the madwoman. It is safe to say that her hand never left her locket during the whole of their stay in the city.

At last, however, the interview was over, though the children had learned nothing about the whereabouts of Pucelle's Heart, and now they seemed to have raised suspicions against themselves. They wore no "cap of Liberty"; they had already been accused of being "Royalists" (whatever that meant); and they took the Harpy's threat to turn them in to the nearest "Section" very seriously. In fact, as soon as the Citizeness left, she walked with a quick and determined step, which made Ada worry.

"Let's get out of here, Lithglib," she said. "I think she's going to turn us in to the police."

"I think you're right," he said. "Let's go." So they continued on down the street, never separated by more than arm's length, and always hiding in shop doors (since they didn't dare go near the guillotine-gates of the houses) whenever a particularly dangerous citizen (or gang of citizens) passed by. All this must have looked very suspicious, but they couldn't help it, so afraid were they. At length, however, they had reason to regret the attention they drew to themselves.

They saw a group of dwarves and goblins, led by Harpy Eighty-Two, coming up behind them. The children moved off to the side of the road to let them go by, but it was obvious that they were coming for them. Ada had never been so scared in her life, watching that gang of armed guards march straight for them, and it took all of her courage not to close her locket and betray her secret.

"You there! You three!" said the chief of the guards, a very nasty looking dwarf. "You're under arrest! You have been denounced for treason against the people and the sovereign republic of Bulverton! Guards, take them away!" With that, they were surrounded, and with a shove, all three children—two dwarf boys and a human girl, to be precise—were made to walk back up the street between their captors, who forced them to go at a brisk pace. Ada was trembling like a leaf. She prayed, but not in words; she was far too frightened for that. If she had been asked what she prayed, she would probably have said, "Dear God, save us!" And you could hardly blame her. Between her fear of being torn limb from limb by Harpies, beheaded by guillotines, cut up into little pieces by dwarves, crushed by giants, and eaten by goblins, it is a wonder that she didn't faint. But she remembered these words: "Do not let your hearts be troubled. Trust in God; trust also in me." (Her parents had, of course, read her the Gospel of John.)

The next half hour or so was a blur, and here her memory fails her. She said it couldn't have been more than an hour between the time of their arrest and the time she found herself sitting in a cart with many other children, rattling on down the road to their execution. She remembers something of a trial, but it didn't last long; and she didn't remember anything the judge said. But that might have had something to do with the fact that both the jury and the crowd—though it was impossible to tell where the one ended and the other began—shouted over the judge, and in the end he was so frightened by the mob that he gave in to their demands. The children had received the sentence of death by beheading. Only one witness was called, Citizeness Harpy Eighty-Two, who denounced the children with the biggest and the strongest words in her vocabulary as enemies of mankind.

So it was that Ada found herself sitting beside many dwarf children (Lithglib and Racket nowhere to be found) in the last of three horse-drawn carts, called tumbrels, tumbrelling, rattling, and rumbling along to her death. Carting, jolting, skipping, and skolping. Rat-a-ta-tabbling, tum-tu-tum-tumbling, tom-ta-tom-tombling. Tumbrelling.

"Someone should really fix these carts," she thought to herself. "Someone should do something about these roads."

She was brought to her senses when a sweet little dwarf girl sitting beside her said, "Are you alright, Miss?"

"Yes, fine, thank you."—which seemed the polite thing to say. The dwarf girl put her dwarf hand on Ada's human hand and never took her eyes off her for the whole trip. She seemed remarkably calm, like Ada's mother. By degrees, she calmed Ada down by talking kindly to her. Ada began to relax and get her head on straight (though probably for the last time). She enjoyed listening to the girl's sweet, small voice. Listening to what she said, though she didn't listen very well, took her mind off her present troubles.

The dwarf girl was one of nineteen other condemned children from the poor district of Bulverton, which was called the Vendée. They remained true to the King. Apart from this, as far as Ada could tell, their only crimes had been being too poor to buy caps of liberty, having unorthodox names, and arranging themselves alphabetically. Their names were Alex, Amanda, Anna Claire, Anna Rose, Betty Jane, Cara, Claire, Dominique, Emily, Jack, Mary, Mary Marshall, Morgan, Morgan Alex, Riley, Ruthie, Sam, Sarah, and Sarah Jane.

As they tumbrelled along, the citizens they passed shouted out, "Vive la Révolution!"

The children shouted back, "Vive la Vendée! Vive le Roi!" and got pelted with angry vegetables and rotten words for their trouble.

It seemed like a hundred years before the town square came into view. From a distance, Ada could see the huge wooden scaffold which the good citizens of Bulverton had built to celebrate their liberty from the King, and the huge wooden guillotine which the good citizens of Bulverton had built upon it to christen their sovereign city with the sort of wine which only their enemies could provide.

Ada took to praying again, and no sooner had she done so than a general cry of panic went up from the city and the carts stopped. People started running back and forth, shouting out fearsome reports: "Monsters! Everyone to the city walls! Defend Bulverton! Giant bugs! Giant pigs! Giant wolves, bats, and drakes! Giant everything! Bulverton is under attack!"

In the end the children were saved by the very evil they had brought with them. The guards abandoned the tumbrels and ran off, although it is doubtful that even a quarter of them went to defend the walls. Most just left their weapons on the ground and ran away like cowards. The children were now at their leisure to climb down from the carts.

It was mass confusion, grownups running this way and that, some stopping to ask the children for advice, most just running in circles, pulling their hair out, and gnashing their teeth. Oh, how they wished the King was there to defend them! Those who said so were called traitors. Others said that there never was a King; it was all wishful thinking. Those who said so were called philosophers.

Ada could find her friends nowhere in the hustle and bustle. The sweet little dwarf girl invited her to come back with her and her friends to their neighborhood, but Ada didn't want to stray too far, in case Lithglib and Racket were looking for her. The dwarf girl (whose name she never got) commended her to the King, blessed her, and wished her farewell, then joined the others as they walked back to the Vendée, singing

Hooray! Hooray!
Vive la Vendée!
Yo ho! Ya ha!
Vive le Roi!
Now dance and sing
And praise the King!
Yo ho! Yo ho! Ya ha!

Soon, however, their *hooraying* and *ya ha*-ing faded away into the roar of the crowd.

Hooray! Hooray!
Vive la Vendée!
Yo ho! Ya ha!
Vive le Roi!
Yo ho! Yo ho! Ya ha!

Ada didn't want to stay in the street for fear of being run over. She saw a quiet stream or river not too far from the road. The afternoon had worn on and lengthened the shadows. In the end, waiting for the right moment to disappear from the crowd, she slipped her locket closed and went to walk by the bank of the river.

CHAPTER TWENTY-ONE

WHEREIN ADA MEETS THE
MAID OF DOMRÉMY

The sun was setting, and Ada walked by the side of the river running through Bulverton, a world apart from the calamity that had befallen the city. Although she never stopped looking for her friends among the general hubbub on the street, all that seemed far away and remote to her. She had a serenity about things now—whether because she had just come out on the other side of a crisis, or whether some magic was at work, she didn't know. It didn't concern her. The peace itself was more important than the reasons for it.

After a while she sat down in the grass and ran her fingers through it. The river chattered alongside her like a friend. It was starting to get a little chilly, but when Ada pulled her hood up and wrapped herself up in her cloak, she was deliciously warm, as snug as a bug in a rug. Even her hunger didn't bother her. She may have dozed once or twice. She may have dreamed.

She was still in that dreamy state and so at first did not believe her eyes, when she saw a little girl in the distance coming toward her along the bank of the river. She was walking slowly, and Ada did not at first see why the sight should have diverted her attention. The girl was short, had long black hair, and wore a midnight blue dress reflecting the color of the water. She had no shoes, but walked barefoot on the green grass, tinted by red and violet light.

Color! The world around Ada was still gray, but wherever this girl walked, there was color. The whole river, too, was now dark blue. The color reached Ada before the dark-haired girl did, and though Ada was still invisible, the other stopped and looked at her.

"Hello," she said, smiling. She had a sweet and compelling voice.

"You can see me?" said Ada, too surprised at the moment to be polite.

"Just as you can see me," the girl replied.

"Hello," said Ada, remembering her manners. "Who are you?"

"I am a simple maid of Domrémy. I serve the King. I keep this river for Him. How do you do, Ada?" She curtseyed.

"You know my name?"

"I know more than that. I know that you search for your friends and the means to heal the evil that has been set loose in the land. More importantly, I know that you are pure of heart. That's why I've come to help you."

"What is your name?"

"I am called Pucelle."

"It must be your heart—I mean, your ruby that we're looking for."

"It is. I will give it to you, but first let us sit down and talk for a while. It has been a long time since I've had someone to talk to. The people of Bulverton have turned to wickedness and forgotten me. They can no longer hear my voice. They have not ears to hear or eyes to see, as you have."

And so Pucelle came and sat with Ada, two girls

visible only to each other, one audible only to the other. If someone had been walking by, he would have heard only one half of a conversation, but he would have seen no one, and he would probably have run away. They chatted, laughed, and chatted some more. Pucelle told her about her wonderful childhood in the country. She had not had the chance to go to school, but she heard the King's voice whenever she was walking by herself.

"I talk to Him too," said Ada.

Pucelle told her of the magic trees and the boundless forests of Domrémy, the feasts, the tournaments, the parish priest, who said a special mass once a year to keep the fairy folk in the forest and out of the town, where their merriment and mischief upset the order of things. She told of haunted glens, church bells at the bottom of lakes, trolls that made you pay taxes to cross their bridges, lucky wells, abbeys and ancient monasteries, and the ruins of dwarves who lived ages and ages ago.

Pucelle also told about how the King called her one day when she was still a young woman and asked for her help. She fought in wars for Him. In the end, she was captured by the enemy and burned at the stake. But they could not burn her heart, so they threw it into the River Sequana. And she'd kept the river for the King ever since.

"The river weeps for His return," she said. "The land cries out for Him. One day, one day soon He will return to His throne, and the people of Bulverton will bow down to Him once more."

"I hope I'm here when it happens," said Ada.

"You wait for Him in your world too," said Pucelle. "Yes, He will come soon. Soon, soon. But He calls all times soon." The girls laughed for sheer joy.

They went on like this until morning, heedless of the chaos into which the city had fallen. Ada drank from the river and was refreshed. Pucelle's water completely quenched her thirst, drove away her hunger, and made her feel like she'd had a full night's rest. It was nearly as wonderful as living water.

At last, however, their time together drew to a close. Dawn sprang up out of the east. Pucelle was telling her a story: "And then, after the priest said his prayer, all the elves—" She stopped mid-sentence and stared off into the yellow sunrise, as if listening to it.

"What is it?" asked Ada. But Pucelle continued to listen. After a few moments, she turned to Ada, and with a sad countenance said,

"The King says it is time for you to go."

"But what about Lithglib and Racket?"

"They will have to follow you when they can. You need to hurry on to Friesland. The evil is just about to reach that kingdom, and their king needs to be warned. I will give you my Heart as well. Good luck and Godspeed, Ada!"

With that, both girls stood to their feet.

"Goodbye, dear Ada! Go down to the river. I have lowered it for you." Ada looked and found that the water had indeed gone down. She could now climb down the bank and stand in the water without being carried away by the current. When she looked back, Pucelle had disappeared.

"Goodbye, dear Pucelle!" said Ada, and then went down to the river. Looking into the water, she saw a bright, red ruby resting among the stones of the riverbed. It shone like a red star, about the size of a quarter, and cast a red light about it. It was like nothing she had ever seen before, and she stood there for a moment looking at it before she remembered what she was about.

Ada opened her locket in order to see better for climbing down into the stream. She saw now that there were flecks of red on her shoes, which she tried unsuccessfully to wipe off on the grass. At last, she climbed down into the river. It was frightfully cold, though the water only came up to her knee. The purifying waters cleaned off her shoes. Ada went to the middle of the riverbed, reached down, and picked up the fiery jewel. She held it up close to her own heart and felt the heat it gave.

"Thank you, Pucelle," she said. At this time, she noticed that the water level had started to rise. It was up to her hips before she noticed. She was startled but knew that Pucelle would never try to drown her. Suppressing her fears, she did not climb out but let the waters rise up to her waist, then to her shoulders, and finally—Ada took a deep breath and closed her eyes—above her head. Oddly enough, she did not float, but stood at the river bottom. She held Pucelle's Heart close, which filled her whole body with warmth, in spite of the freezing water.

Ada opened her eyes underwater and saw Pucelle standing a few feet in front of her. Looking a little sad, she was waving goodbye. At that moment, the current picked Ada up and swept her suddenly and swiftly away. Pucelle, still waving, immediately faded from sight. Although she could not breathe underwater, Ada could hold her breath indefinitely. As long as she was carried along by Pucelle, she did not need to come up for air. She could see quite well too, though she had never opened her eyes underwater at home. The current quickened its pace and carried her quickly but safely downstream, never letting her run into the banks or the bottom. Every now and then a dock or boat flew by overhead. She was now flying with her cloak flapping behind like a cape, going much faster than the current could possibly go. It was exhilarating and terrifying at the same time.

Then all at once the land around her disappeared, and she was out in the open sea, racing like a torpedo or an underwater comet. She flew past huge whales and schools of dolphins, who tried in vain to keep up with her and jumped in the air for joy. Soon, however, the sea darkened in many places because of the huge sheets of ice floating on top. Although the water grew deadly cold now, Pucelle's Heart kept her warm. She was sure to be getting close to Friesland, for she had started to slow down. She wondered how she was supposed to get to land, since the surface of the sea was now one long, never-ending sheet of ice. The only light was a diffused white glow from the sun shining down upon the ice. Ada could now see the sea bottom, and had almost slowed down to the normal speed of the current.

At last her journey was over, and she was now stuck under the ice. She had no fear of drowning, for she could still hold her breath as long as she needed to, but she wondered why Pucelle had left her there. Then she saw it. There was a broad beam of light and a fishing hook coming down into the water nearby. She swam over to the hole and climbed out.

An old dwarf holding a fishing rod and sitting on a stump froze as he saw her come up out of the hole. His eyes were wide, all the color had drained out of his face, and his pipe had fallen out of his mouth. He looked like he had seen a ghost.

Ada, doing her best to suppress her laughter, and failing miserably, asked him which way it was to Friesland. The dwarf slowly moved his hand to point towards land, and Ada giggled her thanks and ran towards shore with her teeth chattering and her cloak pulled tight about her.

— CHAPTER TWENTY-TWO —

WHEREIN FRIESLAND
PREPARES FOR WAR

Friesland was white. Snow weighed on the trees, it floated down in the air, it gathered in drifts and eddies on the ground. The ground was covered with a couple of feet of the soft, dry down of the elements. Ada would have frozen to death if it had not been for her cloak and Pucelle's Heart, which kept her warm even while she was wet.

Ada turned her cloak inside out, transforming it from the greenest green to the whitest white, and put it on again. Now she would be nearly invisible even without the help of her locket. A slow, lazy blizzard blanketed the world in white.

In spite of this, Ada had no trouble finding the road. Frequent use had packed the snow down hard, and the way was marked at every quarter mile by wooden posts surmounted by black, waving banners with the faces of open-mouthed bears painted on. She had been walking for a long time and was nearly dry when she started seeing dwarves on the road. They were all heavily armed and armored, a fierce and warlike people. Dwarves the size of Hyke were a dime a dozen in Friesland, and Mr. Backet would have been the runt of the litter. If she had not been commanded to go both by the Professor and by the King, she would have been too scared, especially after Bulverton. But though the Frisians were a martial race, they were noble. Although they didn't know what she was, having heard neither of humans nor of dryads, they didn't stare. Instead they offered their assistance.

"How do you fare, young one?" inquired one mighty dwarf in dark, shining armor with a great axe on his back.

"Fine, sir," said Ada. "I have a message for the king of Friesland. Could you tell me where I can find him?"

The dwarf looked surprised. "A message for the king of the Frisians?"

"Yes, sir."

"Are you a refugee from some conquered people?"

"No, sir."

"Do you have news of some danger to the Frisians?"

"Yes, sir."

"Come, I will take you to the king." With that, the dwarf turned around and led Ada on the road. She was tired and did not have the strength to go at his pace, and she started lagging behind.

"You are weary from your journey," observed the Frisian. "If it will not shame you, I will carry you."

Ada said that it would not, and the dwarf got down on one knee, removing his weapon to allow Ada to climb onto his back. She did so, wrapping her arms around his bull-neck. He stood up and started off at a jog, holding his axe in his hand. In this way, they went for several miles, the dwarf never tiring or slacking his pace, even though he wore very heavy armor and carried a human girl and an axe as tall as himself. If all the Frisians were so hardy, they would have little to fear from mosquitoes, no matter how big they got. But somehow Ada knew that they would soon have far bigger problems than that. The bear banners seemed to fly by now. Other Frisians looked inquiringly and not without alarm at them as they passed, but her escort never stopped to explain. They passed many houses, all sturdy as oaks.

Finally they reached their destination, a long wooden building whose roof looked like the hull of a boat. The strong-built hall looked like a ship that had capsized. The dwarf set Ada down and quickly addressed the guards at the door, informing them of their errand. Without delay, Ada and her escort were ushered into the hall.

Once inside, Ada saw warriors sitting at benches on both sides of a long table in the middle. Beyond this was a fire whose fumes rose to the wooden beams and rafters and escaped out of vents in the roof. Beyond the great fire was another table with more eminent warriors feasting at it, and at the far end, on a raised platform, sat the dwarf king on his throne. There were wooden pillars running the length of the mead-hall, holding up the roof and separating the central area from the sleeping quarters along the walls.

They entered unnoticed by the feasters, who went on drinking from horns and stripping meat from bone and engaging in bawdy jokes and manly laughter. Ada's escort led her past the long benches to the throne of the king, by far the biggest and most formidable-looking dwarf she had ever seen. He was tall as a man, as broad as three, and more splendidly armored than all. He had a long, black, double-braided beard which came down to his middle, and sharp, keen eyes.

Her escort addressed him thus: "My lord Hrethel, far-famed ring-giver of the Frisians, a child has come with evil tidings for your people."

"Speak," commanded the king, his countenance darkening, and casting a shrewd eye upon Ada.

She gulped hard and began. "I was sent by the Professor," she said, "and a girl named Pucelle who can hear the King—not you, of course, the other King—sir." She was not off to a good start. At the mention of the Professor, the king rose to his feet and the hall fell silent. Ada rallied her courage and began again: "Evil is coming to Friesland, sir. Monsters!"

After this she fell silent too, and the king began to question her. He soon had the whole story out of her— Easelheath, the Calix, forests growing dark, animals growing gigantic, Bulverton. The king and his thanes listened intently to her tale.

When she was finished, the king began giving out orders. One he sent to warn the outlying villages, another he sent to the coastguard, a third he sent to the armory. To Ada's escort (who, Ada now learned, was named Wulfgar) King Hrethel gave the duty of protecting her. She was happy with this arrangement, since she liked Wulfgar, and since she certainly didn't want to be left to herself again, especially if Friesland was about to be attacked.

There was a flurry of activity as the messengers went out, but the king's thanes, already armed, had nothing to do but sit back down to their feasting, though they did so in a much more subdued attitude than before. The warriors were grave and silent, and there was a tension in the room, as if the very air knew that Friesland was on the verge of battle.

Ada was famished, and Wulfgar brought her some food and drink from the table. Ada and her guardian sat off to the side, watching the warriors as she ate. Though Wulfgar had watered it down, the mead made Ada tired and woozy. Wulfgar found her some milk instead, for which she was most grateful. But the mead had already done its work, and since Ada was already tired from her long journey, she soon fell asleep leaning on her guardian.

CHAPTER TWENTY-THREE

Wherein the Mead-Hall
is Besieged

Ada awoke in fear, though she did not at first know why. She found herself curled up like a child in Wulfgar's arms, who was wide awake and vigilant. She turned her head and looked around the mead-hall. All the warriors had left the tables and were sleeping along the walls at full length with their feet towards the mead-benches. Each slept in his armor with his hands on his chest, holding on to his axe. The fire had burned low, and the entire hall now looked like a tomb. Ada started trembling.

Then she heard it: the howling of wolves. This must have been what woke her. It seemed to be getting louder, as if the wolves were getting closer.

"Wulf—" Ada began to say, but he put his hand over her mouth. She wanted to raise the alarm, she wanted to wake the sleeping warriors, she wanted to run away, she wanted to hide. As the howling grew closer, Ada started to panic. It was then that she noticed what she had not noticed before: the king's thanes were not asleep at all. Their eyes were wide open and their hands firmly wrapped around their weapons. One or two gave an involuntary shudder every once in a while which caused his armor to jangle and fall silent. The wolf-din sent a shiver down Ada's spine, and she held her locket tight.

In a whisper, King Hrethel ordered his men to get up

quietly and take their positions. Everyone was now on his feet. The king's retainers stood shoulder to shoulder with their weapons drawn, watching the door. The howling was now right outside, and Ada could see the wolves' swift shadows cast by the moonlight under the door. Huge, monstrous noses started sniffing under the door and huge, monstrous paws reached under it and started digging at the floorboards. The sound of it was so loud that it caused Ada's heart to leap into her throat. She had a sudden impulse to get off the ground.

"Wulfgar!" she squeaked. "Help me up onto the rafters!" He too thought this was a good idea. Ada stood on his shoulders and grabbed onto the lowest beam, then pulled herself up, aided by his hands.

"I'm going to go invisible now," she said to him, "but I'll still be right here." Wulfgar didn't understand, and rather than explain it to him, she simply slid the locket closed and disappeared with a whoosh, leaving her guardian looking up in astonishment. She stood up and waved her hand so that he would see her, but she couldn't tell if he did.

At that moment, one of the king's thanes lost his nerve and ran forward, hefting his axe over his head and bringing it down upon the paw of a wolf. His axe cut off a claw and sunk into the floorboards. There was a great yelp of pain from one of the monsters outside, followed by a series of whines. But that didn't last long. Apparently the rest of the pack was sent into a rage at the smell of blood, because they turned on their companion in a moment and devoured him. Ada could hear the ravenous barking and snapping of the other wolves, but she could no longer hear the injured one.

Ada felt sorry for the poor wolf, but soon she was overcome by fear again, for the rest of the pack attacked the door with renewed vigor. Three, four, maybe five of those infernal dogs tore at it in a frenzy. They thrust their paws underneath the door and raked their claws upon the floorboards, tearing up splinters and ribbons of wood and leaving long scores in the floor. Ada could see their white fangs as their snarling jaws pressed under the door, biting at wood, biting at nothing. The force of their rage shook the door. There was so much pressure on it that the door creaked and groaned, and the crossbar bowed inwards. She was afraid that it would break at any moment and unleash the wolves' fury into the mead-hall.

Apparently the king got tired of waiting. He stood at the head of his dwarves and ordered two of them to unbar the door and let the enemy in. Ada didn't think this was such a good idea, but she didn't have a say in the matter. She loaded her sling and began to whirl a stone. She had picked up a good number of them some time ago, and from her vantage point, and with her skill, she had no fear that she would hit a dwarf. She liked to think that she was now almost as good as Lithglib with a sling. (Hopefully she would see him again.)

On the count of three, two dwarves lifted the crossbar, and the hell-hounds burst into the hall like a flood. Ada was ready for them. She let fly her first stone at the lead wolf, cracking his skull and killing him instantly. His body fell and the other wolves stumbled over him, giving the vanguard time to make the first assault. The dwarves went to work with axe, hammer, and sword. The wolves, after they recovered from the first shock, went to work with tooth and fang. Ada went to work with her sling. She focused especially on the wolves around the king, and there was nary a one that she did not kill or blind while her ammunition lasted.

These wolves, as I have said, were much bigger than normal wolves. They had dead, white eyes and long black hair which looked and moved like spider legs. The demon dogs barked, snarled, lunged, and chomped at the dwarves' armor, while the Frisians in turn broke, hacked, and cleaved their way through the canine flood and swept the wolves from the threshing floor of their wrath. There were many deaths, and wherever a body fell—from either side—thither came the wolves. In eating the dead, they were distracted from the living. Nevertheless, things were not going well for the dwarves. Many warriors had fallen, the king himself was injured, and more wolves came in to replace the dead ones—or to drag bodies from the hall. Wulfgar was nowhere to be found. Ada was out of ammunition. The dwarves were losing ground, being pushed back toward the throne.

Now all that was alive beneath her were wolves. Though they could not see her, they could smell her. The wolves began to jump up at her. Ada had never been so afraid in her life. The infernal dogs leapt so high that they nearly nipped her toes. She held on to an angled beam, terrified that she would fall off or that one would find her foot or the end of her cloak and pull her down into the pack. She prayed harder than she ever had before. Some of the wolves fell into the fire, but in their madness, they continued to jump at her.

Ada couldn't take it anymore. Nearly dancing on the beam for fear of the devouring maws, she looked around among the rafters. Above her was a vent through which she could see the stars. If she could climb up to it, she could get out onto the roof. Because of her small size and her long limbs, she was a good climber, and she was fairly sure that she could climb the slanting beams without falling. She was paralyzed by fear, however, because of what would happen to her if she did fall. She opened her locket so that she could see better to climb. Her appearance, if possible, sent the wolves into an even more violent rage than before, which caused her to hesitate. She did not try to climb until the rafter beneath her feet shuddered at the impact of a wolf body. Now she was off the beam and climbing, suspended in the air, hanging on to the sloping beam above with her arms and legs wrapped around it. She felt something fall out of her pocket, but she did not dare try to see what it was. She could not hang there forever, and she knew it. Soon continued up through the rafters, and at last—at long last—she was out upon the roof.

The night air was sharp and cold, and her first breath of it caused her to cough after the hot fumes of fire and slaughter below. She was shaking like a leaf, but not because she was cold. The stars shone out in the sky, pinpricks of heaven in the black shroud of night, and she longed to be among them. She sat on the ridge at the top of the roof, feeling a bit shipwrecked. When she looked out upon the village, she saw more battle going on below, and on the other roofs, dwarf-women and children.

Ada wept and offered up many inarticulate prayers. She prayed for the Frisians; she prayed for herself, that she might find her way home at last; she prayed for Lithglib, that he might never know the full extent of the evil he had let loose into the world. She implored the King, the One King, to save them. She did not know what to pray for on behalf of those who were already lost. This question was foremost in her mind, and raising her eyes to heaven, she asked God what could be done.

At that time, Ada heard a still, small voice inside her, as sweet as Pucelle's, as comforting as her father's.

It said, *Do not let your heart be troubled, little one. Trust in God. Not one of my children shall be lost. Your light and momentary troubles are achieving for you an eternal glory that far outweighs them all. If your earthly body is destroyed, you shall have an eternal body in heaven. Though outwardly you waste away, inwardly you live. Meanwhile you groan and are burdened, because you wish to be with me in your heavenly dwelling, so that what is mortal may be swallowed up by life. Therefore, always be confident and know that as long as you are in your earthly body, you are away from the Lord. You prefer to be away from the body and at home with me. So make it your goal to please God, whether you are at home in the body or at home with the Lord. For all must appear at the judgment seat, that each one may receive what is due him for the things done while in the body, whether good or bad. Do not lose heart, little one, for I tell you the truth: All shall be well, all shall be well, and all manner of things shall be well.*

Ada let these words wash over her.

Are you satisfied?

"Yes, Lord," said Ada, and waited for the dawn.

CHAPTER TWENTY-FOUR

WHEREIN A KING IS LAID TO REST

Ada had not had a proper night's rest since Brickworks, and it was starting to wear on her. Many a time she nodded off and nearly rolled off the roof. That would have been disastrous, for even if she survived the fall, the wolves were still below, though now fewer in number. The battle raged on till morning, when finally the dwarves won, though not without heavy (and bitter) losses. At first light, Wulfgar (as Ada learned afterwards) found her perched precariously on the ridge of the roof, sound asleep. He took her to his own house and laid her in his own bed, an angel in a white cloak. He himself stood guard at his door and waited for the sounds of her stirring.

When Ada awoke, it was well past daybreak. The brisk, Northern light was coming in from the window and resting on the bed. Ada found herself alone in a room with a small fire going, trapped under the warmest and heaviest—or rather, the only bearskin blanket she had ever felt. In her present state, it took some effort— both moral and physical—to get out from under it and find out what had become of the world in her absence.

The moment she was up, she heard Wulfgar's footsteps. He stopped outside the door and asked if he could enter, and upon receiving an affirmative answer, a black and blue Wulfgar came in with her breakfast:

milk, cheese, and bread. He moved stiffly and had a lot of swollen, bruised, and discolored bite marks.

"What happened, Wulfgar!"

"Victory is with the dwarves," he replied in a weak voice. "But the king—he is not expected to live out the day."

"You should have woke me up!"

"Finish your breakfast, little one, and we will go to him."

"I'm finished now," she declared. She drank her milk in two draughts, stuffed the bread into her pocket, and stood ready to go. Wulfgar didn't argue with her. Instead, he led her out. Once outside, Ada was a little more subdued. The marks of the previous night's attack were everywhere. Widows wept for their husbands, orphans for their parents. The bodies of wolves were being carted off, as Ada found out, to the far border of Friesland to be pitched into a ravine. The bodies of dwarves were carried on litters to a deep underground vault, where they would be laid to rest by the bones of their fathers. Fences, gates, walls, and doors all needed to be repaired. It was a dark day for the Frisians.

Wulfgar led her not to the mead-hall, which was still being cleaned, but to the king's private quarters. Ada would not have been able to find them on her own, for the king's house was not much more remarkable than those of his subjects. When they entered, they found a wounded king lying on a huge bed with his wounded warriors standing around it. He had obviously had the worst of it (as good kings always do). He had already lost the power to move and the power to speak, and was now slipping in and out of consciousness, although apparently he had been asking for her; for shortly after her entrance, a very ancient she-dwarf got up and came to her.

"Let's talk outside," she said in a kind, old voice, putting her hand on Ada's back as they turned to go. Wulfgar supported the dwarf-woman with his arm as she walked, and helped her down the step.

The dwarf-woman turned to Ada but did not speak at first. Grief and kindness were competing for mastery of her face, but kindness won out in the end, although her lips quivered and there was a tremor in her voice. Ada teared up.

"My son wanted to talk to you," she began, "but he has lost the power of his voice. He told me of your errand, brave child, and what necessaries you require from the Frisians to heal the evil in the land. Tomorrow I shall have them for you. The myrrh is ready at hand, but I shall have to send dwarves to collect the flax from the mountain side. We seldom have need of such things, but I fear we shall have need of them today."

Ada didn't understand this last remark but didn't have the heart to ask her about it. The three of them returned to the king's bedside. His eyes were closed, but he was still breathing, with difficulty. He continued to draw breath until the sun reached the zenith of the sky and started his descent; then the king expired. The people wept for him and began preparing his body for the grave. Ada, though in a state of shock, took note of the fact that they wrapped his body in a white, linen robe, which of course was made from flax, and anointed it with perfume, which of course was Frisian myrrh. The last two elements which the Professor asked for—she did not dare ask herself why—were used to prepare the dead for burial.

When the king's body was ready, the dwarves carried it out on a bier. Ada and her guardian followed the procession.

On a cliff overlooking the sea, the Frisians built a huge pile of straw and wood and laid King Hrethel's gigantic body upon it. Upon this pyre, Wulfgar said, they were about to burn their king. This was a little unsettling to Ada, who had never been to this kind of funeral before.

Her attention, however, was momentarily diverted to a ship which had been hauled up on shore far below. However it came about, on that side of Friesland the sea was not covered by a sheet of ice. Rather the waves and the water went out all the way to the horizon. There was a harbor down below, on the coast of which lay the ship. Though it was far away, Ada could see dwarves attending to it.

"That is the king's ship," Wulfgar said, noticing her glance. "The Frisians will launch it unmanned upon the water when they see the signal fire."

There were more things going on around the pyre, and Ada and Wulfgar now turned towards it. The king's mother, too feeble to make the journey on her own, had been carried on a litter and gently seated on a chair some distance from the mound. The Frisians were piling treasure around the body of their king: Gold, garnet, and silver; brooches, belt fittings, bangles and rings; bear-crested helmets; ivory drinking-horns teaming with gold, beakers full of coin; pommels, hilts, torques, and necklaces; huge coats of mail; bridles and trappings; iron axes, iron hammers; runic blades and battered shields—all were heaped upon the funeral pyre, bound to be burned with their lord. A wail went up from the dwarf women, a long lament for their fallen king. Who now would lead the Frisians? Who would protect them from their enemies? They foresaw the destruction of Friesland once and for all. More wolves and evil things would come. How would they be saved? They were lordless, hopeless! So they made their grief, while the warriors stood silently by and watched the newly kindled flames lick their way through the sticks and straw and rise to consume their king. Ada was crying. A fierce, Northern wind blew the flames into a red heat and set the whole pyre ablaze. A crackling, sizzling ruin. The worst defeat Friesland had ever suffered. How indeed were the Frisians to be saved? They had no hope unless the world was set to rights again! Now, more than ever, Ada understood the urgency of her quest.

"That was a good king," said Wulfgar, and nothing more, though Ada could tell that his sorrow was deep. It darkened his face and wrinkled his brow, but it did not soften his features. Rather it hardened them. Not to worry: Ada wept enough for the both of them.

The wind came in occasional and spontaneous blasts. The flames roared and gave off so much heat that Ada and others were compelled to take a few steps backward. The blaze melted the snow around the pyre and sent up a huge pillar of black smoke as well as a great quantity of ash, which mingled with a gentle snowfall that had just begun and came down upon their heads. Ada put her hood up, for among the flakes of snow and falling ash were sparks and bits of flaming debris. Her tears ran down her cheeks and made little holes in the snow at her feet.

The king's ship was pushed into the water and drifted out to sea. The mourners remained until it disappeared over the rim of the world and night closed in around them.

CHAPTER TWENTY-FIVE

WHEREIN ADA RETURNS
TO BRICKWORKS

That night the king's mother insisted that Ada and her guardian stay with her—"for company," she said, but Ada suspected that it was at least as much for her own benefit (and her safety, for the warden of the snow-lands was no more). She got a warm bath, a hearty meal, and a full night's sleep. In spite of their loss, the Frisians held her as a kind of local hero or prophetess for warning them of their danger. They waited on her hand and foot, though with a certain degree of vigilance, as if they expected the attack to be repeated the second night. It wasn't, thankfully. Ada fell asleep with her head on the old mother's lap, listening to stories of great deeds King Hrethel had performed in his youth. Wulfgar carried her to her bed.

The next day Ada was anxious to resume her quest, especially because all throughout the day reports came in about trees falling down in the forest and village dogs going mad and having to be put down. But unfortunately the mountain was far away, and the dwarves who had been sent out for flax did not return until nightfall. They came into the old mother's house with a bag full of the rare blue flowers for Ada. The old mother, in turn, gave her a full measure of myrrh in an ornate, blue glass bottle in the shape of a bulb. It was icy to the touch. Ada accepted these things with a heart full of so many different emotions that I don't know how to describe it.

No sooner had she thanked them than a report reached the house that something unusual was happening in the mead-hall. The old mother's guards drew their weapons in alarm, but the messenger said that no enemies had been seen.

"Some kind of magic is at work," he said.

Accordingly they all followed him out into the dark, with all the queen-mother's warriors about her. It was a cloudy night and there was no star to be seen, so Ada held her locket up to her eye and looked through the lens as they walked. While they were still some distance from the hall, Ada saw light shining out of the door, though it soon faded to nothing. But a moment later, the light grew bright again. With her other eye, Ada could see that the light was red, too red to be fire. It waxed and waned in this manner until the party had come right up to the door of the mead-hall.

Then it occurred to her. "I think I know what it is!" said Ada, taking a step forward.

"Are you sure, child?" said the queen-mother.

"Yes, ma'am; I'll be fine." With that she entered the hall, which had been purged of every trace of the battle, except for some dents and cuts in the wood, which she could only see when the red light filled the room. It was coming from somewhere in the middle, right under the rafters which Ada had climbed. She soon found the source. Sure enough, it was Pucelle's Heart, glowing like a distress beacon. This must have been what had fallen out of her pocket.

She bent down and picked it up. When she stood up, she found Pucelle standing in front of her.

"Well done, Ada!" she said. "You've done well here, but now you must return with me—quickly!—to Brickworks. The world will not last much longer if the chalice is not restored!"

"I'm ready!" said Ada.

"Go down to sea." After these instructions, Pucelle disappeared with the red light, and Ada put the ruby back into her pocket. She walked out with the aid of her locket.

"Who were you talking to, child?" asked the old mother.

"Pucelle, ma'am," she answered. "I have to go down to the sea and return to the Professor. I've got everything we need to fix the Calix!"

"But there are no ships, dear; and even if there were, you couldn't very well set out in the dark."

"Oh, we won't need any ships, ma'am."

"Well," said the queen-mother, "I trust you know your own affairs. Goodbye, brave girl! Godspeed! And may your errand succeed—for all our sakes!"

The other Frisians wished her farewell too, except for Wulfgar, who escorted her down to the harbor, the very harbor from which the king's ship had been sent off. Though she could not see it, the Frisians had built a tremendous mound of dirt over the site of their lord's cremation. They named it Hrethel's Barrow.

It was a long way down to the harbor. When they reached the bottom and stood on a rock over the deep water, it was time to say goodbye.

"How will you go, fair one?" said Wulfgar, with the first sign of tenderness in his voice. "Will you disappear again?"

"No," said Ada. "I think I have to jump into the water."

"You'll freeze. You'll drown."

"I'll be fine. I've done this before."

He seemed uncertain. "Why do you hold that to your eye?" he asked.

"So I can see in the dark. My eyes aren't as good as yours."

After a moment, he said, "Farewell, Ada. May we meet again, in this world or the next."

"Farewell, Wulfgar." She pulled him down and gave him a kiss on the cheek.

Now there was nothing for it but to jump into the arctic waters in the dead of night. Wulfgar looked like he was ready to jump in after her. Finally she worked up the nerve, held Pucelle's Heart in both hands, and plunged into the water. A colder shock she had never received in her life, but the instant she sunk beneath the surface, she was swept away from Wulfgar and Friesland. Unlike before, she did not gain speed slowly, but instantly flitted off like a shooting star. But as before, as soon as she was underwater, Pucelle's Heart filled her with warmth. She was rushing west now, so fast that she was catching up with the sun. The light began to return, so that by the time she returned to the continent, there was still daylight left. By ways unknown to her, Ada was propelled to the very streambed which ran by Mr. Lillipupan's house. She could see the roof of his shack when the waters began to recede and left her standing on dry ground.

"Go invisible, Ada!" said Pucelle, who had appeared next to her. She was right, for though Mr. Lillipupan's shack remained the same as ever—although now boarded up—the rest of the world had become something of a nightmare. In the failing light, Ada could see that the trees had turned as black as charcoal and their leaves were gone. All the little woodland animals had grown to gigantic size and taken on a sinister aspect. Here a bird had dead, white eyes; there a squirrel had spidery hair; there again a beetle the size of a Labrador! And the flying insects!

Ada vanished and followed Pucelle, who ran on ahead of her, though she left no footprints. Ada, on the other hand, was bogged down by the mud. But soon they were running through the woods. Every vine, every root upon which Ada's foot fell tried to wrap itself around her ankle! If she stopped for a moment—or worse!—if she fell, she would never go another step. If she had dared to look behind her, she would have seen several monsters picking up her trail and sniffing after her, some of them so hideous and deformed that she would not have been able to guess what animals they used to be. She ran as hard as she could, and Pucelle led her aright.

At last, bursting through the trees, Ada crossed the border of the black forest and stumbled onto the grounds of Brickworks. She saw the house in front of her, with its evening lights just beginning to come on. She was safely within the magic boundaries of the estate.

CHAPTER TWENTY-SIX

WHEREIN MANY
THINGS ARE REVEALED

As Ada approached the house, she made sure she had all the necessary ingredients. Pucelle's Heart? Check. Frisian Myrrh? Check. Linen? No, but she had the flax to make it. Calix? That was still with Lithglib, wherever he was. Sage? Not a clue. Oh well, they couldn't expect her to do everything.

She was so happy that, even though time was short, she decided to play a joke on her friends, a joke which, as a rule, all possessors of magic jewelry play on their friends at least once. She decided to sneak up on them. Ada went invisible. She walked through the garden and right up to the front door, and slipped in.

Everyone was having dinner. Everyone! There was Lithglib, Racket, the Professor, the Professor's wife, the Major, the Secretary, the Gardener, the guinea pig, Professor Tobit, Mr. Field, Mr. Hill, the prodigious Dr. Humpty, and Mr. Lillipupan. Mr. Lillipupan! Yes, the world had grown so evil, even he couldn't live in it. In the end, as Ada was to learn, he was forced to take refuge at Brickworks. And of course, though they were very surprised, they could not turn him away. They were very patient with him, though there had never been a more ungrateful guest, or a worse dinner companion. You see, Mr. Lillipupan had always wanted to come to Brickworks, but only after accepting an invitation to join the Professor's literary club—as his equal, but really, his superior. But to come under such conditions! to be forced by the necessity of his own safety! to be driven from the very world he was working to create!—it was an indignity too great to endure. And he never let his hosts forget it. He folded his arms and sat in angry solitude. Every attempt by the staff to offer him refreshment was met by an incredulous stare. Every attempt to make conversation with him was answered by contempt. Every question put to him was met by a petulant reply, or by silence. Every attempt, even on the Professor's part, to be civil with him ended in frustration. The Major took to calling him Sir Mopes-a-lot, or when he had been drinking, Sure Mopes-a-lot. Mrs. Clark took to calling him nothing at all, but made sure he was never alone with the silver.

And so, for one reason or another, dinner was a silent and sullen affair. Hardly anyone looked up from his food. Hardly anyone spoke, except to ask for a dish. Lithglib looked the gloomiest of them all. Apparently it had become a habit for him to stare off towards the door, because for a moment Ada thought he was looking at her. But of course he was looking past her, into some great distance only he could fathom in the depths of his despair. She would have to make this quick.

Surely, if their heads had not been hanging over their plates, someone would have seen the phantom of a girl climb onto the table, but no one did, except perhaps the guinea pig. Ada stood in the middle of the table, looking down at the melancholy eaters, and almost gave herself away by a giggle.

She wanted someone to mention her name, so that she could say, "And here I am!" and appear in their midst, like in the movies. But it didn't look like that was going to happen, and she wanted to break up their pity party as soon as possible. So instead she said in a loud voice, "WHY SO GLUM?" and appeared with a whoosh! Their surprise was so great that several people fell back in their chairs, including Dr. Humpty, who had to be helped up by Mr. Field, Mr. Hill, Mr. Wolper, and Mr. Ford.

"Ada!" they cried, looking up at her in astonishment.

"We thought you were dead!" said Lithglib, helping her down from the table. Ada hugged him. The next several minutes were ones of great excitement and rejoicing, and everyone participated except Mr. Lillipupan, who, after the initial shock of her appearance, sank back into his chair and his self-imposed isolation.

A place at the table was set for Ada, although she didn't get to eat much, since everyone wanted to hear her story. Before she began, she put the three items the Professor had asked for on the table, which was an even greater surprise than her reappearance.

"How did you survive Bulverton?" Lithglib asked. "We thought you'd gone to the guillotine."

"The carts stopped before we got there," she answered. "I waited for you guys."

"That happened to us too!" said Racket. "We looked for you, but we couldn't find you in either one."

"'Either one'?" said Ada. "There were three."

"Not in our group," said Lithglib. "There were only two carts in ours."

"The guillotines are very busy in Bulverton," said the Professor ironically.

Mr. Lillipupan humphed, but no one paid him any attention.

"I waited for you by the river," said Ada. "Where

did you guys go?"

"To the Vendée," said Lithglib, "the only normal neighborhood in Bulverton. We went back with other people who escaped."

"I almost went there. I meet some children from there too. How did you get back to Brickworks?"

Lithglib looked ashamed. "We waited for you as long as we could, but Bulverton was being attacked. There's probably not much left of it now besides the Vendée. We slipped out during the fighting."

"And almost didn't make it back!" Racket cut in. "There were lots of monsters!" He gave an involuntary shudder.

"But how did you make it out of Bulverton, Ada?" said Lithglib. "And how did you get all these things?"

"I met Pucelle down by the river."

"Met her?" the Professor inquired.

"Yes, she's very nice. She keeps the river for the King. Anyway, she knew all about us and our quest. She gave me her Heart and sent me to Friesland. I went underwater—really fast! The Frisians gave me the other things, then Pucelle brought me back here."

She hadn't explained very well. The exact mechanics of her transportation through the water were a mystery to the others. Nevertheless, the Professor asked,

"Did you meet the king of Frisians?"

Ada's countenance fell. "Yes, sir," she said darkly.

"What's the matter?" he replied with some alarm. "Didn't he treat you well?"

"It's not that, sir. He's—he's dead, sir."

"Dead!" cried Professor Tobit. "King Hrethel is dead! How did this come about!"

"The wolves attacked. I'm sorry, Lithglib, I didn't want to tell you. The evil has reached Friesland. Things are just as bad everywhere as they are here!"

All the color drained out of Lithglib's face. Ada had thought that he could not sink any lower, but she was wrong.

"Then we haven't a moment to lose," said the Professor. At these words, the faces of the other adults at the table darkened. They obviously knew something she didn't. The Professor continued: "Mrs. Clark, you know what to do with the flax. I shall take the other things and begin my work."

"What about the Sage, sir?" said Racket. "Don't we need him?"

"The Professor is the Sage, child," said Professor Tobit.

"WHAT!" cried all three children at once. Ada stared openmouthed. Lithglib was stunned to silence.

Racket said, "Why didn't you tell us, sir?—if you'll forgive my manner of speaking. I didn't mean to imply that you should have."

The Professor smiled, though his joviality was subdued. "What would you have done if I had told you?"

"Nothing, sir."

"Precisely."

CHAPTER TWENTY-SEVEN

WHEREIN THE FINAL PREPARATIONS ARE MADE

The next morning Lithglib was not at breakfast. Ada, who had earned a good long sleep, was the last to come to the table.

"Where is Lithglib?" she asked with some alarm.

"He went outside," said the Professor (or the Sage, or whatever we're supposed to call him now).

Ada ate a quick breakfast, excused herself from the table, and went outside to find her friend; and the first thing she noticed was how dreadful the world was—even in daylight. The trees outside Brickworks were so dark that it looked like a forest fire had reduced the surrounding woods to cinders. The limits of the estate were so well defined that it was as if someone had drawn a line around the perimeter—within the circle it was green; without, black.

And so it was not without fear that Ada saw Lithglib in the distance, sitting on the ground a short distance from the western boundary, facing the woods. All the time that Ada walked towards him he never looked around nor turned his head. It was as if he had been turned to stone. This apprehension did not go away when she actually came up to him, for she found that his face was ashen gray and so cadaverous that he hardly looked alive. She was scared to touch him. She was also scared of the woods, for more than once she thought she heard a rustling sound or caught a glimpse of something moving out of the corner of her eye, but whenever she looked she saw nothing.

"Are you all right, Lithglib?" she asked.

He made no answer. Ada tentatively put out her hand and touched his arm. It was cold and hard, though not as cold and hard as stone. It was still flesh. At her touch Lithglib moved his head ever so slightly toward her. After a moment he spoke, though his voice was so low that she barely heard him.

"I was just thinking," he whispered, "about home. I was wondering if anyone is left."

Once again Ada didn't know how to console him. She couldn't tell him that she was sure they were fine, for of course she wasn't. And she couldn't tell him that it was not his fault, for of course it was.   But if you have ever known someone who was grieving, someone who has lost a loved one, then you probably also know that it is often best to say nothing at all. Sometimes your company is the only thing that gives him any comfort, and gives him a great deal more comfort than you know.

So Ada just sat there and prayed for him silently. They remained still for a long time, Ada trusting in the Professor's magic to protect them from the evils without, and trusting in the King to protect them from the evils within. At long last she thought she saw some of the color return to Lithglib's face and his features relax a little bit.

Luckily there was work to be done, and soon Lithglib was called away from his brooding. Mr. Ford had come to call the children back to the house. There they found the Professor and Racket waiting for them, and soon the three children were following him down the hill towards the hot air balloon.

As they walked Ada began to notice something running along the ground. It looked like a silver thread when she looked at it at a certain angle; otherwise it was invisible. It looked like it was running from the house to the balloon. Ada stooped and picked it up.

"Ah, I see you have good eyes, child!" laughed the Sage.

"What is this for?" said Ada.

"One end of it is tied to the chalice, the other to the balloon. When once we've got the Calix working again, you won't be able to touch it, so this thread will carry it with you to Easelheath."

The cord was as thin as gossamer but cold and unbreakable, and it was visible only when it caught the light just right. The boys said they could see nothing.

"What is it made of?" Ada inquired.

"No common material, I can tell you that. The distaff side of the family" (by which he meant Mrs. Clark) "made it from the sound of a cat's footsteps, the roots of a mountain, and the breath of a fish. It is made from impossible things; so, naturally, it is impossible to break."

Soon they reached the hot air balloon. The balloon part of it was full and the basket was moored to the earth by means of several ropes staked in the ground. Every once in a while the mechanism above the basket gave a short burst of flame (all by itself!) to keep the bag filled with air. The Professor explained that the balloon was enchanted in order to take its occupants wherever they wanted to go.

"Why don't you just use the controls?" asked Ada.

"I don't know how it works," he confessed.

After that Ada was called away to help Mrs. Clark with whatever she was doing. Ada found her in the attic working at a vertical loom. The linen threads (more than Ada thought it possible to make from what little flax there was) we m a beam and stretched taut by clay we To Ada, the whole process was a b of spindles and heddles, warps a d that she would not be much use to had never learned how to weave at h e, however, that she was only there t since the dwarf woman seemed to ne nce she seemed a little sad.

"What are you doi Ada asked to announce her presence.

Mrs. Clark instantly seemed to come out of the mild sorrow in which she was momentarily indulging and to compose herself. "I'm passing the skein through the warp," was all she replied.

"Interesting," said Ada politely. Then, when it didn't look like she was going to say any more, Ada volunteered, "How did you make so much out of so little, ma'am? And how did you do it all so quickly?"

Finally Mrs. Clark smiled. "You don't suppose my husband is the only one with a little magic around here?"

"I guess not." Ada smiled back.

But now it was Ada's turn to be troubled. As the morning and then the afternoon wore on and turned to evening, she realized what it was that Mrs. Clark was making. It was a robe—no! it was a burial robe, just like the one which King Hrethel had worn. It was beginning to dawn on her what the other two elements which the Sage needed were for. Frisian myrrh had been used to anoint the king's body. She had known this already, but had not dared to ask why such things were needed to repair the Calix. Now she could no longer avoid the conclusion: Someone else was going to die! But who?

The answer came to her from Mrs. Clark. "My husband," she said, holding up the finished robe and struggling to keep her voice in check. "My husband—please take this to him."

Mechanically, Ada took the robe from Mrs. Clark and walked with it at arm's length to the Professor's study. His wife, her work finished, stayed behind.

When Ada entered, she found the Sage, Lithglib, and Racket seated by the fire.

"Ah, I know my wife's work when I see it," said the Professor. He meant to say this with levity, but his heart was too heavy. He met Ada in the middle of the room and took the robe from her. Ada, a little white, went and sat down next to Lithglib without a word and fixed her eyes on a dirty spot on the carpet.

The Sage slowly put on the robe, and the conclusions which Ada had drawn came much faster to Lithglib.

"Wait, sir," he said. "What are you doing? Do you mean to say that this is the only way the Calix can be fixed?"

"I'm afraid so," he replied.

Poor Racket was left in the dark. When Ada glanced up at him, she saw confusion and fear on his face.

A few moments of silence passed, and then finally Lithglib lost his composure. "No, no, no, NO!" he cried, rending his hair. "No one else is going to die for my crime! I broke the Calix! I brought about all this evil! I deserve to die! Let it be my life! Please!"

"I'm sorry, son," said the Sage. "That is a very noble sentiment, but I'm afraid it simply doesn't work that way. Your death wouldn't do it."

"But I did nothing to help! I couldn't even get the things to fix it! I couldn't even protect my friends! I have done nothing! Nothing but evil! Why can't I just do this one thing!"

Lithglib was inconsolable. Rather than answer him immediately, the Sage came to him, put his hand on his back, and let him weep.

When he was a bit calmer, Lithglib said, "Please, sir, I need to understand."

The Sage sighed and smiled on him, then spoke these words: "It takes a sage or a king to repair a broken world. Thus it was decreed by the One King. According to rumor, there are worlds in which He has reserved that right for Himself, and in which He has already made such a sacrifice. Moreover, the cup cannot be repaired by the hand that destroyed it. Do not be upset that I say this, Lithglib, for I say it neither out of anger nor out of judgment. You have already repented of your crime and received the King's pardon, though you little know it and, I fear, accept it with great difficulty. Do accept it, Lithglib, for there is no other way for you to be free of your guilt. The King Himself has granted you pardon, and He knows far better than you the extent of the evil you have done. He is wiser than you, wiser than all, and if He grants you mercy, you would be a fool to reject it."

Inexplicably, Ada was moved to speak. "It's okay, Lithglib," she said. "It's the same in my world. We've all done bad things there and need the King's pardon. The Sage was right: He did come to our world Himself and died to save it! We messed everything up, but there was nothing we could do to fix it. The King offered free pardons to anyone who would accept them, but some people don't—I don't know why—but don't be like them!"

Lithglib sat in silence for a long time with his eyes fixed on the carpet. And after what seemed an age, he lifted his head, seemingly for the first time since Ada had known him. He looked at the Sage and at her.

"Thank you, sir, and thank you, Ada. I understand now. I accept the King's pardon."

CHAPTER TWENTY-EIGHT

WHEREIN A SAGE IS LAID TO REST

"And now, children," said the Sage, "I wonder if you would join me in the garden this fine evening?"

They said that they would and followed him out. The moon was bright and big, and the air was cool, which, combined with the fresh smells of the garden, filled Ada with a pleasure that was as much like sorrow as it was like joy. The Sage trembled a little, and Ada took his hand.

"Thank you, Ada," he said. "I must speak with the King. If you three would wait for me here, I would be grateful." Thus the Sage went off by himself to pray, and Ada and the dwarf-boys sat on a bench in the moonlight. The night was majestic; fireflies glowed about the garden. The Sage was away so long that the children grew drowsy. When Ada awoke, she felt guilty for falling asleep and wondered what the Sage would think. Lithglib's head was bowed and his hands were folded, as if he were praying in his sleep. Racket's head hung to one side, and he was leaning in such a way that he was about to fall off the bench. Ada had been sleeping with her head on Lithglib's shoulder, but now she sat up and looked around alertly for the Sage. Had he already gone in? Had he seen them asleep?

Ada got up from the bench and walked slowly around the garden. He was not far away. Ada turned the corner of a hedgerow and found him on his knees, very close, clasping his hands and looking up toward the stars.

"O King!" he cried in a hoarse whisper. "If you are willing to take my place, do so! If not, give me courage to do what must be done!"

Ada had frozen, but after he spoke these words he noticed her.

"I'm sorry!" she said. "I didn't mean to spy on you. We fell asleep, and I thought maybe..." She left this sentence unfinished.

"That's all right, child. I was just about finished anyway. Will you walk me back to the house?"

Ada supported him with her arm. He seemed to have aged a hundred years in an hour, he was so weak. He trembled a little every few steps. Ada was ashamed of the dwarf-boys when they came up to them, still sound asleep. She cleared her throat loudly just like her mother did whenever she was doing something she wasn't supposed to.

The boys woke up with a start—only then did Racket fall off the bench—and apologized profusely to the Sage. Then all four of them went back into the house. Ada passed the old dwarf on to his wife, who was waiting up for them, and then everyone went to bed. That night Ada heard rumblings as of distant earthquakes, which caused her to offer up silent prayers for Easelheath, Friesland, the Vendée, and all the dwarf kingdoms of the world. If only they could last just a little longer!

No one spoke at breakfast the next morning. They hardly even ate. Lithglib was sad, but his sorrow was mingled with gratitude, and he was still free from his former guilt. The Major was more sober than he had ever been, and (probably for the first time in his life) had woken up before the lady of the house. Professor Tobit looked grim. Even Mr. Lillipupan looked sulkier than usual. The Sage fasted.

Ada knew this was his last day. She had hoped that the morning would last forever, but after everyone had finished breakfast (though no one got up from the table), the Sage finally said,

"Well, we had better get started; the world out there is not getting any better," and stood up from the table.

There were a few final instructions to be given. The Sage led them outside to the oven attached to the house. Ada could feel the heat coming out of it and smelled the smoke; its chimney was working dutifully. Now Ada could see the silver thread disappearing into the kiln.

"The chalice is inside the oven," he said. "Once I am gone, it will be restored. All you have to do is get into the balloon. Don't dally too long, for the magic of Brickworks will not last long after I depart. Good luck, children, and Godspeed!"

At last there was no putting it off any longer. Everyone assembled in the large, museum-like room beneath the stairs. Someone had removed the center display and put a big, stone table in its place. The Sage, still wearing his linen robe, which now smelled strongly of myrrh, got up and lay at full length on the slab with his hands crossed on his chest. Mrs. Clark, full of sorrow and quiet strength, sat beside him with her hand on his, leaning over him.

Some had already started to cry, but of all present, it was Mr. Lillipupan who spoke first:

"You can't be serious, Clark!" he burst. "A man of

your qualities throwing your life away for weaklings and fools! Think, man, about all that we could achieve together! We could rule!"

The Sage calmly replied without turning his head: "It is a far, far better thing that I do than what you propose, Mr. Lillipupan. It is a far, far better world that I leave behind than what would be if I remained."

Mr. Lillipupan was silenced.

Ada was relieved to find it was not to be a sudden or violent death, nor even a painful one. The Sage faded away much as King Hrethel had done, though with no wound, no poison, no natural means of any kind. If there had been any doubt of that, the manner of his death would have settled the question once for all. Over the course of several minutes, with his wife looking down into his eyes with a fixed smile and softly caressing his hands, the Sage's breathing grew lighter and lighter, until Ada did not see his chest expand any more, though she could not recall the moment it ceased to rise. Whether this was the moment of his death or whether it came sometime afterward, Ada could never determine, for she was so fraught with sorrow, joy, grief, gratitude, and a hundred other emotions, that she was not much use as an objective observer. What she was certain about was that after some time, the color of the Sage's skin—no, his whole body! including his clothes, started to change. It grew gray and moved no more. No breeze would ever again stir a hair of that noble head. No hand would ever flatten the creases of that noble robe. All was stone. All was stone.

Ada heard Professor Tobit explain, "That dwarf was of high, gnomic blood. From stone we were made, and to stone incorruptible some of us return, if it pleases the King."

The Sage was fixed forever in the position in which he lay, a reclining statue of gray marble, now shining in the light of the sun coming in through the shutters. Mrs. Clark's smile was also fixed in adoration for her blessed husband, and she had stopped caressing his hand. In fact, she too had stopped moving entirely. It took some time for Ada to find this remarkable.

"Mrs. Clark?" she said at last with some alarm, but the dwarf woman made no answer.

Professor Tobit, overcome with mourning, did his best to answer: "Mrs. Clark had been ill for a long time, child. She would have passed on long ago if it had not been—if it had not been for him. He took some of her pain upon himself, and so helped carry her burden. This is the King's own magic, and none but his truest sons can wield it." Mr. Lillipupan looked as if he had taken this last remark to heart.

At that moment, however, there was a loud noise outside, which caused everyone to rush out, leaving the incorruptible bodies of the Sage and his wife in their everlasting pose and eternal rest, where—for all I know—they sit to this day and where—for all I know—they will remain until the One King decrees that that world shall come to an end and be gathered up again to Himself.

CHAPTER TWENTY-NINE

WHEREIN THE WORLD IS SET TO RIGHTS

When Ada and the dwarves rushed outside, they heard a loud hissing sound and saw a huge pillar of steam rising out of the kiln chimney and more pouring out of the loading window. Soon, however, it was not just steam pouring out, it was water! Real, glorious, blessed, living water! It poured right out onto the ground and bathed their feet. They cupped their hands under the oven opening and caught up some of the magic water to their lips. The real thing was better than Ada's memory of it. How it filled her heart! How it filled her soul! All the evil and suffering of the past few months (or however long it had been) were washed away. It was all worth it. Ada was satisfied.

Lithglib was a new dwarf. She hardly recognized him, so happy he was! Racket was back to his giddy old self again. The Major had a new favorite drink.

Even Mr. Lillipupan was in rare form. He had, he said, an idea of rebuilding Bulverton. A town like that could use a dwarf of his talents. After all, it was founded by his great uncle, Ezekiel Bulver. Perhaps he would start a club of his own. He would call it the Revolution Society. "I wonder if Dr. Price is still knocking about," he said. He was in such high spirits that he condescended to tousle Racket's hair, give him an affectionate slap on the back of the head, and go inside to pack up his things (including, curiously, the silver).

There was only one momentary trouble which interrupted their mirth. The magic that kept Brickworks safe was gone.

"Look!" cried Ada, though she could not conjure up the appropriate fear at the moment. The blackness of the surrounding forest was coming towards them. The dark grass was closing in on the house in such a way that it looked like a giant had spilled his bottle of ink or like an army of ants was attacking. Monsters would soon discover that the magic barrier was no more. But the water was spreading outward from the kiln at the same rate, enlivening the green of the lawn as it went. Ada and the dwarves watched to see what would happen when the wave of black met the wave of green. It was no contest. Green won. The instant that death encountered life, it was swallowed up by it. The curse retreated before the nourishing virtues of the Calix, and a fecundity of opulent verdure overcame the creeping shadow. Soon the whole plain was alive and dazzling. It was like something out of a dream. Ada watched the black trees in the distance throw off the coils of death as color returned to them from the bottom up. From trunk to bough to the ends of branches, life returned. Like a speeded-up film, the trees sprouted fresh leaves, an explosion of emerald green. Ada wished she could have seen the transformations of the animals back to their natural forms, but the first glimpse she had of their redemption came when a deer took its first tentative step into the meadow and the birds took to the air and their song again. A more magnificent fantasia of life Ada had never known, and it brought tears of joy to her eyes.

She was not alone. The others were overjoyed by

the sight, and expressed their elation alternately by awed silence and ecstatic cheers. But their work was not yet finished.

"We have to go now, Ada," said Lithglib. "We have to take the Calix back to Easelheath. From there it will restore the whole world!" They took their leave quickly from the adult dwarves, who wished them well and blessed them with full hearts, and the three children ran laughing down the hill with their cloaks (two green ones and a white, to be precise) fluttering behind them in the wind.

When they reached the bottom of the hill, they raced up to the hot air balloon and climbed into the basket. The moment they were all in, the burners fired, the balloon rose into the air, and the ropes fell away. They waved to the dwarves below as they were carried over the house. Ada saw the Calix fly out of the kiln and follow the balloon, seemingly (at that distance) attached to nothing. The dazzling silver chalice was drawn up until it was only about twenty feet below the basket, trailing after it through the air. From that distance, Ada could not pick out which jewel was Pucelle's Heart; it must have turned all the other gems red. Ada wondered whether Pucelle was still linked to her Heart or whether she had gone to be with the King like the Sage and his wife. She was never able to find out, because she was not allowed to touch it.

Soon, however, Brickworks and the other dwarves faded from view and the children were flying over the black forest west towards Easelheath. But the overflowing cup continued to pour life into everything below. Following and keeping up with the hot air balloon was a tidal wave of green which shot out to the north and the south and healed everything it touched. It was a breathtaking sight. The whole world was being righted before their very eyes. Trees burst into blossom as they passed; birds shed their black wings and lifted up their song. The only things which the water did not heal were the enormous cracks and fissures in the ground where the earth had fallen in. Those would probably never be closed. These must have been the result of the rumblings which Ada had heard the night before. She prayed that no dwarf villages had been lost into the earth.

She wondered about some of the people and places she had seen on her journey, and as if in response to her silent wish, the balloon took her past some of them on their way back. The dark castle where the goblins lived had been swallowed up by the earth. The balloon took them over the gigantic crater where it had once stood. Ada could not say she was sorry for it.

Later that day, for the hot air balloon moved with surprising speed, they came to the golden meadows— that is, they became golden again as they passed—and saw a herd of buffalo in the distance. All three children strained their eyes to see their giant friend, but this was unnecessary, for the balloon carried them right over him, low enough that they could shout and wave to him. The giant, who at first had remained stock still at the approach of the flying machine and the wave of color it brought, gestured and bellowed joyfully when he recognized them. He had obviously been able to defend himself and his bison during the ordeal, and he was uncharacteristically animated after the strange and wonderful shower which he received as the balloon went over his head. After that the burners shot two long jets of flame into the balloon until they regained their former altitude.

At last—at long last!—Easelheath came into view!

This was the darkest spot they had seen, which filled them with dread at what they might find there; but by the same token it was the greatest contrast when the Calix brought new life to the region. There was the acid lake—now purified! There were the giant mosquitoes—soon shrunk to the size of ordinary pests! There were the reported firebats, hovering like a cloud of flame over the smoldering treetops—quenched! There at last was the empty village, the mansion, the boulder houses, the stone circle, the Fountain itself—now full of color and light again! They passed right over it.

"Why didn't it take us down?" asked Ada.

"It's taking us to Calix Pond," Lithglib replied. He was right. Soon the trees opened up to a very ordinary-looking pond, or rather a hollow, since presently it contained no water. In the center of the hollow was what looked like a single, white, Roman column. The balloon slowed to a stop right above it and sunk until the Calix gently came to rest upon the top. At this point the magic thread must have disappeared, because when the balloon rose again to return them to the village, the chalice was left standing on top of it, rapidly filling up the pond—rapidly filling up the world!

"Goodbye, dear Pucelle!" said Ada.

As the balloon rose, there was now no part of the world as far as the eye could see where the curse still lingered. All was as bright and alive as the day Ada first came into the world.

CHAPTER THIRTY

WHEREIN THE LAST
GOODBYES ARE SAID

The hot air balloon touched down in Easelheath within the stone circle a short distance from the Fountain. The three children clambered out, whereupon the balloon rose again and floated off to the east from whence it had come. Racket waved goodbye to it before he realized how ridiculous it was, not that that would have stopped him.

They now eagerly hoped things would return to normal. The ivory Fountain was still silent, but it was sure to erupt with life any minute. There was a question of whether they should wait there for the villagers (assuming there were any left) or whether they should go look for them. There was also a question of whether Lithglib should make himself scarce until it could be determined whether Easelheath was going to forgive him.

Both questions where soon answered, however, by the arrival of the citizens of Easelheath. They were a wretched lot indeed, the thinnest and most harried band of dwarves the children had ever seen. While a good number of them came huddled together down the road from the elder's mansion, many of them seemed to spring up out of the ground, whether by grass-overlaid hatches or by spade. All had lean and hungry looks, all blinked at the garish light of day, all looked more like hunted animals than people. They just kept looking around doubtfully, as if waiting for something horrible to pounce on them. Every now and then two of them would bump into one another or be startled to find each other so close and nearly jump out of their skins. It might have been funny if it had not been so associated with recent events.

Nevertheless, Lithglib steeled himself for whatever was to come. From whatever hole or rock they emerged, the citizens of Easelheath naturally seemed to gravitate toward the Fountain. At first no one recognized the adventurers with their fine weapons and clothes, but recognition returned when they collected their wits. Naturally, the dwarf-boys were looking among the gathering crowd for Hyke and the Backets, though they remained where they were. But thankfully, they did not have to wait very long, because the dwarves, though certainly grateful to be able to see the sun again, began pointing at Lithglib and muttering amongst themselves.

"Lithglib!" cried his father all of a sudden, emerging from the crowd and coming to embrace him. Although the least miserable-looking of all the dwarves, Hyke had obviously lost some weight and had seen battle, for he had bruises and scars, and his arm was in a sling. Mr. and Mrs. Backet recognized their son before he recognized them, for they had lost so much weight that they looked like different people. They had a hollow and feeble look about them. Ada had a strong and unaccountable urge to cook them dinner, which she did that night. They had no words left; instead Mrs. Backet simply threw her arms around her son and began blubbering. Mr. Backet stood patting his son on the back with a fixed scowl of approval.

Ada was happy for them, but she hoped the Fountain would start again soon, because the villagers began to find their voice:

"Isn't that the boy that started all of this?"

"It is."

"Wasn't he banished?"

"He was."

"And yet he's returned?"

"He has."

"And the punishment for that is death?"

"Indeed it is."

"Then where are the soldiers?"

"Here." This last voice belonged to one of the aforementioned warriors, although he was so weak with hunger that he seemed rather weighed down by armor than wearing it, and his axe was not carried so much as dragged. Nevertheless, he was soon joined by others, and it looked like they were about to have a fight on their hands. But at that moment the Fountain intervened. After a momentary tremor in the earth, the water burst like a geyser into the sky and rained down upon their heads before resuming its normal height. The taste of living water upon their lips put everyone into a better mood.

"That changes things, doesn't it?"

"I don't know, does it?"

"Where is the chief elder? He knows these things."

"I'm here."

"Then answer the question."

The chief elder paused for a moment. "Well, according to the rule of postliminium, a banished dwarf who makes restitution for his wrongs may be readmitted into the community." Many dwarves wondered if there was any such law on the books, but there certainly was the next time anyone bothered to check. At any rate, with the restoration of the Fountain and their homes, the citizens decided to throw Lithglib a party (instead of an execution).

Many other things were said and done, all of them happy, and there were many kind words and many stories told. The children spent the rest of the week with their parents, except Ada, of course, who spent it with her friends' parents. But by this time she felt a strong desire to return home, since her stay had been a little longer than she had originally planned, and since she was afraid that by this time her parents had given her up for dead.

Lithglib, Hyke, and the Backets had all come to see Ada off at her tree.

"Goodbye, dear Ada," said Lithglib. "I'm sorry I never finished your song. I promise that it will be a good one and will be passed down in Easelheath for as long as the world lasts!"

"Goodbye, little dryad," said Mr. Backet in an exceptional moment of feeling. "We give you thanks for your assistance here."

Mrs. Backet hugged her mightily. "Goodbye, deary!" cried the she-dwarf, who had already regained some of her former weight and all of her former strength.

"Yes, goodbye, dear Ada," said Racket, after his mother had released her. "Do come again. We promise you'll have a nicer visit the next time. If you don't mind my asking, what are you doing with your fingers?—not that it's any of my business."

"Counting," she said, with tears welling up in her eyes.

"What are you counting?" Lithglib asked.

"The number of friends I'm leaving behind." Eighteen. Eighteen was the number she reached. Nineteen if she counted the giant. Twenty if she counted him twice.

At that she lost it. Ada burst into tears and hugged her friends. She had a strong feeling that she was never going to see them again. In the end, she gave them back their things, including Diana's Locket, which was hardest to part with.

"Are you sure you don't want it?" said Hyke. "It was a gift, not a loan."

"I'm sure," said Ada.

Now there was nothing left to do or to say, and they had no more excuses to postpone her departure.

"Let's try this one more time," laughed Lithglib, wetting his squeegee with holy water and raising it to the tree. Everyone held their breath, but when he swiped the tree with it, a window into Ada's world streaked open. Everyone exhaled.

"I guess this really is goodbye," said Ada. "I love you all and will miss you dearly." The feeling was heartily reciprocated.

And so Ada climbed through the window and returned to her own world. A pale light was just beginning to break over the horizon, waiting to guide her home. Ada would not find out until she got back that it was the only the first morning since she left. So little time had passed in her own world, so much in the other! Ada turned around and waved to her friends one last time before Lithglib, with a look of sorrow mixed with joy, wiped the window away with a streak and a squeak. So ends Ada's adventure of the window in an unlikely place.

WHEREIN THE NARRATOR CONCLUDES HIS TALE

By the time Uncle Daniel finished telling his tale, Ada and the twins were in tears, not because it was sad, but because it was happy.

"Tell us another story!" Andy and Melissa cried.

"I'm afraid that it is time to go," said Uncle Daniel. "I see that your car is all packed up and your parents are waiting for you."

They were overcome with despair. "But what will we do now?" they cried.

"There are plenty of good books to read, much better than the story I told you."

"Would you make us a list?" asked their parents. "We'll stop at the library on the way home."

Since Andy and Melissa were not likely to get a better deal than this, they decided to be satisfied. Uncle Daniel pulled out his pen and notepad and started writing a list of his favorite books "for young'uns."

"This should tide you over for now," he said, and handed it to them with a smile.

Then Ada said, "And what about me, Uncle Daniel? Can you write down some books for me?"

Uncle Daniel wrote another, longer list of books "for old souls," as he said, and tore it out of his notepad.

"And how about us?" asked Ada's parents. They had heard parts of Uncle Daniel's story during the course of the vacation as they were coming and going, and wanted to know what kind of books he recommended for adults. Uncle Daniel made a third list and handed it to them. (You can find all three of these lists at the back of this book.)

Andy and Melissa were gone, and now Ada's parents were telling her that it was time to go. She had thought that by the end of the vacation she would be begging to go home, but now she was slow to leave.

"Thank you," said Ada to Uncle Daniel, holding on to his list like a treasure. "For the story, I mean. Thank you for the story. If you write it down, will you send it to me?"

"As you wish," he said with all the love in his heart. She had a strong impulse to hug him, but she didn't. Ada left him to help her parents finish loading the car. Little did she know it, but she left her magazine by the fireplace. There it would remain until the next fire. Somehow she also managed to lose her smartphone, which first caused her pain, but after a while, relief. Her parents noticed a marked improvement in her character, too. Thereafter Ada began referring to these kinds of things as "bad spells," much to her friends' bewilderment, and to Uncle Daniel's favorite books as "good spells," much to her friends' disdain. But she did happen to find her chapstick—it was in her pocket, of all places!—and that was something.

In any event, the car was now packed and Ada had run out of excuses to stay. She paused before going downstairs for the last time and looked at Uncle Daniel, who was sitting by the window. If she had known it would be the last time she would see him, she would certainly have run and thrown her arms around him and told him how much she loved him. But she didn't, and it has never quite sat right with her. The last time Ada ever saw Uncle Daniel, he was sitting in an armchair, reading *The Divine Comedy*, chuckling to himself.

Uncle Daniel's Favorite Books

— For Young'uns

C. S. Lewis	*The Chronicles of Narnia*
J. R. R. Tolkien	*The Hobbit*
George MacDonald	*The Princess and the Goblin*
	The Princess and Curdie
Lewis Carroll	*Alice in Wonderland*
	Through the Looking Glass
J. M. Barrie	*Peter Pan*
Robert Louis Stevenson	*Treasure Island*
Elizabeth George Speare	*The Bronze Bow*
Madeleine L'Engle	*A Wrinkle in Time*

— For Old Souls

C. S. Lewis	*Out of the Silent Planet*
	Perelandra
	That Hideous Strength
	The Great Divorce
	The Screwtape Letters
J. R. R. Tolkien	*The Lord of the Rings*
[Anonymous]	*Sir Gawain and the Green Knight*
Charles Dickens	*Great Expectations*
	David Copperfield
	A Christmas Carol
William Goldman	*The Princess Bride*
Sir Arthur Conan Doyle	*The Complete Sherlock Holmes*
Alexandre Dumas	*The Count of Monte Cristo*
Jules Verne	*20,000 Leagues Under the Sea*
James Hilton	*Lost Horizon*
Harper Lee	*To Kill a Mockingbird*
[Anonymous]	*Beowulf*
Dante	*The Divine Comedy*
Homer	*The Iliad*
John Milton	*Paradise Lost*
Virgil	*The Aeneid*
Charlotte Brontë	*Jane Eyre*
Jane Austen	*Pride and Prejudice*
Snorri Sturluson	*The Prose Edda*

Edwin A. Abbott	*Flatland*
Dorothy Mills	*The Book of the Ancient Greeks*
	The Book of the Ancient Romans
	The Middle Ages
Jonathan Swift	*Gulliver's Travels*
John Bunyan	*The Pilgrim's Progress*
John	*The Gospel According to John*
Luke	*The Gospel According to Luke*
	The Acts of the Apostles
Solomon	*Proverbs*
Sean McDowell, ed.	*The Apologetics Study Bible for Students*

— FOR GROWNUPS

C. S. Lewis	*The Abolition of Man*
	Mere Christianity
	Miracles
	The Weight of Glory
	God in the Dock
	Christian Reflections
	The Problem of Pain
Dorothy Sayers	"The Lost Tools of Learning"
Douglas Wilson	*The Case for Classical Christian Education*
Neil Postman	*Amusing Ourselves to Death*
	Technopoly
	The Disappearance of Childhood
Elizabeth Kantor	*The Politically Incorrect Guide to English and American Literature*
Peter Kreeft	*Socrates Meets Jesus*
William Lane Craig	*Reasonable Faith*
Lee Strobel	*The Case for Christ*
Gregory Koukl	*Tactics*
Paul the Apostle	Epistles
Ted Cabal, ed.	*The Apologetics Study Bible*
Mortimer Adler	*How to Read a Book*
Encyclopaedia Britannica	*Great Books of the Western World* (1952)

46144993R00122

Made in the USA
Lexington, KY
24 October 2015